SHORT STORIES BY IAN P. OLIVER

DELAYED
REACTION

An anthology of desire

SHORT STORIES BY IAN P. OLIVER

DELAYED REACTION

An anthology of desire

MEREO
Cirencester

644 8691

Mereo Books

1A The Wool Market Dyer Street Cirencester Gloucestershire GL7 2PR
An imprint of Memoirs Publishing www.mereobooks.com

Delayed Reaction: 978-1-86151-352-6

First published in Great Britain in 2015
by Mereo Books, an imprint of Memoirs Publishing

The address for Memoirs Publishing Group Limited can be found at
www.memoirspublishing.com

The Memoirs Publishing Group Ltd Reg. No. 7834348

The Memoirs Publishing Group supports both The Forest Stewardship Council® (FSC®) and the PEFC® leading international forest-certification organisations. Our books carrying both the FSC label and the PEFC® and are printed on FSC®-certified paper. FSC® is the only forest-certification scheme supported by the leading environmental organisations including Greenpeace. Our paper procurement policy can be found at www.memoirspublishing.com/environment

Typeset in 10/16pt Century Schoolbook
by Wiltshire Associates Publisher Services Ltd. Printed and bound in Great Britain
by Marston Book Services Ltd, Oxfordshire

Contents

Delayed Reaction

The dipped headlights cut a silvery wedge through the inky darkness. Harry Tristen's leather-gloved hands gripped ever tighter around the steering wheel as he pushed further down on the accelerator pedal. Every now and then a white signpost passed him by, but he knew the turn-off; she had pointed it out on a map to him on countless occasions. Perhaps a mile down the country road on the left was the signpost he was searching for: LITTLE THORPE MANOR ½ MILE. Harry flicked on the interior light and checked his watch; he was ten minutes late. Just a half mile now and, as the road narrowed, part of the headlight beam rendered the outline of the building in silhouette. It looked eerie and forbidding.

Jenny Deschamps sat in the drawing room sipping a gin and tonic. The drink had been designed to relax her nerves, but it had the opposite effect of stiffening them. Even the way she perched herself on the edge of the chair, crossing and then uncrossing her legs, said it all. Any other night she might be relaxing, mixing with friends and passing pleasantries, clad in a dinner dress, possibly even a ball gown. But tonight it was a checked shirt and Levis. There was a silk bow pinned to her golden hair that spilled over her shoulders with an electrifying bounce. She wore no make-up. She possessed that natural beauty that many a woman would pay thousands to achieve under the surgeon's scalpel.

She glanced over at the grandfather clock again and confirmed the time on her wristwatch. Where was he?

She rose and made her way over to the bay window, drink in hand. She pulled back one of the velvet curtains. Her reflection revealed anxiety, a mirror of personal foreboding. There was only blackness out there but for several ground-level floodlights which illuminated the front lawn. An owl hooted in some distant fir tree.

He pulled up slowly at the huge wrought-iron gates and switched off the headlamps, keeping the sidelights on, engine purring quietly. These steel barriers, in that moment, became an instant reminder of time, the incarceration, the locking away from society because he wanted to be rich. Forgetting that black spot in his life, he quickly lifted the mobile and dialled a number.

'Come on, come on,' he muttered.

'Harry?'

'Yeah, it's me.'

'It's the side entrance by the double garage.'

'Gotcha!'

He slipped the mobile into his shirt pocket. Then the gates opened automatically, at which point he edged the car forward and drove up the winding driveway in first gear, the only sound audible being that of the crackle of car tyres on stone chips.

The driveway took him up past the front door to the east wing of the mansion and the double garage. Harry, fortyish, with tightly-trimmed black hair, bold forehead and arrogant jaw with just a hint of suntan, stepped out of the BMW. He sneaked around the path which separated the house from the garage and approached the side entrance. As he raised his hand to rap on the door, it opened suddenly, cautiously. Jenny stepped to the side and allowed him entry.

They kissed as only lovers do, his embraces finding her waist and bottom, with hers concentrating on his hair and neck. There had been two long, lost weeks since they had seen each other last, and it was demonstrated now in this spontaneous flurry of passion. They parted, their eyes exploring each other.

'How are you, my love?' Tristen asked, his eyes never leaving hers.

'Fine... fine, I guess,' she replied.

'You're nervous, aren't you?'

She sighed deeply. 'Of course I am, Harry. You can't expect me to be delighted, over the moon, wanting to tell the whole world about it, can you?'

He pulled her tighter towards him. She revelled in his raw strength. 'No no no. I'm sorry, I should be respecting you more for what you are doing. And I do respect you, Jenny. You know that, don't you?'

Her lips almost managed a smile. 'Yes, Harry, I know that.'

'And I'll always love you, Jenny.'

She took her eyes off him for a moment and shivered. 'I'll always love you, Harry, no matter what happens.'

'I'll tell you what's going to happen, Jenny. We're going to spend the rest of our lives together. And what's more, you'll have the family you've always wanted. I just can't wait to be a father.'

Jenny gazed into those dreamy eyes of his and said, 'Oh, Harry, let's have lots and lots of kids. It would be a dream come true, it'd make my life complete.'

Tristen eased away from her. 'You sure you don't want to change your mind?'

Jenny turned away as they entered the hallway and looked up at the winding staircase. 'No, Harry.'

She clasped his hand tightly and led him towards the staircase. The stairs were fitted with a wine-coloured deep pile carpet. On the wall hung ancestral portraits of the Deschamps family stretching back 400 years. Tristen momentarily reflected on the impending termination of such grandeur. They stepped onto the first landing, where an errant breeze resulted in the tinkling of a crystal chandelier directly above them.

'Along here,' Jenny whispered.

The corridor was dark and there was a coldness about the place. Jenny stopped at a door, which was slightly ajar, and made a gesture with a forefinger to her lips. She opened the bedroom door and tiptoed inside, Tristen stepping tentatively behind her. The only light in the room came from bedside table lamps and the two VDUs. They hummed and bleeped, along with the buzzing of machines that resembled hi-fi equipment. There were snakes of cables and tubes, electrical wiring, what looked like oxygen bottles and respirators. Pervading all this was a distinct antiseptic smell.

The huge white bed sat in the middle of all this, and from their distance, the only evidence that a human being was occupying it came from an oxygen mask. They approached the bed.

'Will he be able to hear us?' Tristen whispered.

'No,' Jenny replied also in a whisper. 'He's been like this for a month. It's just a matter of time, according to Dr Lyon. Could be days, months, years. Who knows?'

They were at the bedside table now. Tristen couldn't keep his eyes off the oxygen mask and the drawn, wrinkled face, the haunting, rhythmic wheezing. His eye caught one of the VDUs and he watched the luminous, jagged lines as they passed horizontally across the screen, ostensibly indicating the vital signs of a vegetable.

Tristen took in the air. 'Shit, this place smells like a chemist's shop.' Noting the vacancy in her eyes, he tugged on her arm. 'Let's go, Jenny. Look, I hate to say it but maybe we're doing the old boy a favour.'

Still gazing down at her husband, she said, 'He scares me looking like this. It's as if he knows about us and all this is some madcap ruse to get at me.' She paused for a moment. 'Come on, Harry.'

Downstairs, Jenny switched on the lights and closed the double doors of the drawing room behind her. Harry did not know where to look first. The walls were covered from top to bottom with bookcases, Persian rugs and tapestries, every chair and table of Edwardian style, in every corner ivory carvings of Eastern origin, and taking pride of place, the white Italian marble fireplace.

'Impressed, Harry?'

He picked up a brass ewer in the shape of a lion and viewed it curiously. 'And what the hell is this?'

'It's an aquamanile. It's fourteenth century. Samuel picked it up in Paris five years ago.'

'Pretty.'

'He is... was... forever buying things on a whim. Whatever took his fancy.'

'And how much did it take to... get you?'

'Cheeky bastard. I gave that man years of happiness. You could even say he worshipped me.'

'I can believe that, Jenny, but it's us now. We've got to look to the future. Now, where's the safe?'

Jenny moved quickly over to the wall beside the fireplace. She pulled out the hinged water colour to reveal a shiny steel door. 'It's all yours, Harry,' she said. Turning abruptly, she went over to the window and pulled back the curtain. She made another cursory check outside. By now Tristen was at the safe, twiddling with the calibrated dial.

'And it's all in here?' he asked, with a mischievous grin.

'Yes, Harry,' she replied nonchalantly, 'twenty-five million at the last count. But how do we get rid of it?'

'My contacts in Amsterdam are ready and waiting. They've got buyers lined up. It's a piece of cake.' And with a corny American twang, 'It's just you and me, honey.'

'Harry, we haven't much time left. Now, the combination. It's twenty-five left, thirty-two right, fifteen right, forty-seven left, twenty-six right and forty-three left.'

Tristen sniggered. 'You'll never believe this but that combination is almost identical to a job I did in the Republic of Ireland years ago. This is the first time in my career I've actually been given the combination. Yeah, it was the IRA, Jenny. It was a cinch as well. I'll give it to them, they were a real organised bunch of shitfaces.'

'You didn't tell me about that, Harry. You could've been killed.' She sighed. 'No more jobs after this one. Right?'

'Scout's honour,' he replied, saluting her. She left him with one of those long, admiring smiles.

He commenced to rotate the dial, whistling as he did so - nope, there was no problem here. The dial he turned this way and that, always knowing what was behind the steel door: unbounded wealth, freedom from two-bit gangsters, the knowledge that he could spend the rest of his life with Jenny Deschamps, the first time in his life he could say with great aplomb that he was his own man.

Forty-seven left... twenty-six right... yup, he'd finally arrived. He'd soon have money coming out of his ears and treat himself to that Roller he always knew he'd own one day. Forty-three left...

Jenny, with her hand on the drawing room door, witnessed the explosion. It knocked over a vase of pink

7

carnations on one of the bedside tables in the room where Samuel Deschamps lay.

Detective Sergeant McKay, getting on for retirement and balding, with a temperamental twitch about his moustache, and Detective Constable Richardson, twenty-two, wearing that kind of babyish face that did not belong to an officer of the law, surveyed the blackened and charred room. Forensics and other specialist officers were going about their duties. One man, the police photographer, was finishing off his scene-of-crime photography.

'The sprinkler system seemed to be quite effective, sir,' Richardson said.

'Didn't help him, Richardson,' McKay replied, nodding to the black polythene body bag. 'The intruder, whoever he was, didn't stand a chance.'

'I've never seen anything like it,' Richardson stated.

'You've got a lot more coming, Richardson. Once you're involved in cases where heads and limbs are missing, then you can say you've moved up a notch.'

Richardson picked up the aquamanile, resembling now a battered-up old kettle. 'They seem to be into antiques in a big way, well, what's left of them.' He noted the woman entering the room. 'Sir,' he said, with a nod of the head, 'here's Mrs Deschamps.'

Jenny was clutching a handkerchief and touching it around her nostrils. Arriving beside the two policemen, she glanced at the body bag and immediately looked away.

Detective Sergeant McKay said, 'I'm... we're terribly

sorry about your husband, Mrs Deschamps, but if it's any comfort to you, I would suggest that it was the force of the blast which cut off his life support systems. Mind you, it's only speculation. Terribly sorry.'

'But I don't understand,' she declared, puzzled. 'The safe. Why the safe?'

'That's in the hands of forensics, Mrs Deschamps,' McKay replied. 'As for him over there,' he continued, scratching his head, 'it's how he got in, that's the question. There's no sign of forced entry either upstairs or down. The alarm systems and CCTV are in perfect working order.' He looked directly at Jenny when he offered, 'Of course he may have had a key.'

'You're not suggesting...'

'No, Mrs Deschamps, I'm not suggesting anything.'

McKay noted the woman's interest in the body bag. 'He wouldn't have felt a thing, Mrs Deschamps, which is just as well. If he'd survived, his face would've needed extensive reconstruction.'

Jenny slumped onto the settee and broke down. The tears flowed and they were genuine, perhaps the first expression of personal integrity in her life since meeting Harry. Maybe relief, in that this insane merry-go-round of deceit, had come to this. Happiness, she contemplated, was as futile and transient as the charred and dented aquamanile at which she now gazed.

'Well, Mrs Deschamps, I think we've done all we can for the moment,' McKay said. 'Two deaths in one day is enough for anyone.'

'I'll be okay, Sergeant,' she said. 'Time is a great healer, they say. No doubt I'll get over it.'

Charles Vorster, Samuel Deschamps' solicitor, reclined in a button-backed armchair and adjusted his reading glasses. On his desk was a laptop computer and two CDs. A letter lay next to an opened envelope. Sitting opposite were Jenny Deschamps, Detective Sergeant McKay and the family doctor, Arnold Lyon. Jenny sat on the edge of the chair, smoking a cigarette, every now and then turning to glance at the policeman. Why should he be here? And if this was supposed to be the reading of the will, why was the rest of the family not invited?

Then she gave some thought to the fact that nearly all the contents of the safe had been destroyed by the explosion. Harry, the only man she had ever truly loved, was dead, and to the authorities, he remained unidentified. The police had not at this point asked for any statements from her about that fatal night, so she had had time to contrive some extraordinary tale to explain how he had entered the house. During her love affair with Harry she had developed a wealth of excuses, devising believable situations to explain the endless days she had spent at his flat, engaging in torrid love sessions that went on for hours. But now, now in this baleful hour, she knew nothing would ever bring Harry back.

'Mrs Deschamps, gentlemen,' Vorster said firmly. 'Firstly let me thank you for coming around this morning. And, Jenny, allow me to extend my deepest sympathy. Sam was a true friend of mine, as you know.'

'But Charles, what is this all about?' Jenny asked.

'Exactly. Why do I need to be here?' demanded Dr Lyon.

'Very well. I have two CDs here,' he began. He held up the letter. 'This letter accompanied the discs. It contains instructions. The first CD I have listened to, as instructed by Mr Deschamps.' He pushed the disc towards McKay. 'You, sir, will need this later. This other CD I was to play in front of you three, again as instructed by Samuel...'

He was interrupted by Jenny. 'Oh, this is preposterous!'

'Jenny, please, I think we should leave the last word to your... husband, ' Vorster replied.

The solicitor slipped the disc into the laptop computer and clicked the mouse. The three listeners simultaneously edged forward on their chairs. There was a moment's silence before the croaky voice began.

'The following is an account of the circumstances leading to the unfortunate death of myself and my loving wife, Jenny.' The latter glanced curiously at Vorster. Samuel Deschamps, deceased, continued. 'I have to confess that I knew of my wife's affair with one Harry Tristen, but I chose to turn a blind eye to it, as it were. An old man like myself could hardly provide - how would one put it - a physically romantic association with her. My health was deteriorating by the day and you, Dr Lyon, will attest to this fact.' There followed an outburst of violent coughing. He continued in a chesty murmur.

'Her naivete was touching to say the least, her beauty an everyday blessing, but the family honour had to come first. Her indiscretions are well documented in the other disc, the dossier of which was compiled by a private detective. I took the step of contacting a security consultant, who shall remain anonymous, who was instructed by myself to wire an explosive device inside the safe to the fuses governing my life support systems. This was carried out at the point where I felt I would either die or become comatose. It would seem a bitter irony that I should decide on such extreme action. But I had to ensure that we would leave this bitter, twisted world together. Jenny, by the way, was the only other person who knew the combination to the safe.

'And now I am with my love in that eternal paradise which distinguishes not between the emaciated body I endured for so many years and the beautiful woman I married. We are now as one. God forgive me.'

A single tear ran down Jenny's cheek. Charles Vorster turned his laptop off, closed it and sat staring at Jenny Deschamps. An utter silence bathed the room in which they sat.

Still gazing rigidly at the laptop computer, she uttered painfully, 'Harry, I am so sorry. That was meant for me.'

The Caller

Alison sat at the phone, rolling a cigarette. The 'skins' were slightly damp, which made sticking the papers difficult. But as usual she had great trouble completing the task, such was the nervousness that not only ran through her hands but through her actual veins.

Having successfully put together the roll-up, she rummaged through her handbag and found a book of matches. On lighting the roll-up she went into a drawer of her desk. The half-bottle of vodka was finished. In a fit of despair, she threw the bottle into a metal bin in one corner of the desolate 'office'.

'Fuck it!'

The telephone buzzed. It was a stare of intimidation. But she knew she had to answer it, to once more go through the filth, the sordidness that went with the job. Having cleared her throat, she sat poised and upright.

'Hello,' she began in that forced, sultry, enunciation which was so practised and well-honed. 'I'm Rosy. Who do I have the pleasure of talking with? Hmmm?'

'Pleathe, pleathe say you'll meet me tonight. I have thomething I want to thow you,' the voice declared, almost suicidal in its desperation.

'I've told you before, whoever you are, just fuck off and leave me alone...' The door to the office opened. '...and if you don't I'll get somebody to fix you proper.' She threw down the receiver.

A tall, skeletal figure, with bald head and eyes that looked like tiny glass beads, stood by the side of the desk. He was dressed in an impeccably-cut pin-stripe suit. He leaned over Alison.

'And just what the hell do you think you're doing? Look, darlin', the punters come first, you second. Get it?'

'It was that maniac again, Jake,' she said wearily. 'He's fuckin' weird. A real nutcase.'

'They're all nutcases, sweetheart. Some of them are perverts. But then we're in the business of perverts aren't we? Those are the ones that pay our wages. Right?' She couldn't stand to look at him. 'Right?'

He clasped his hand around her chin and turned it around. She smelt the stale alcoholic breath. She almost vomited, not so much because of the smell, but from to having to eke out a living in this sordid and corrupt world of his. Yet in some ridiculous, quasi-professional sense, she regarded herself as a sex therapist, as if she had the credentials to pacify and please her callers.

'Now, you be a good girl, and when that phone rings again, you just make sure you do the business, or you know what?' He dug into his inside jacket pocket and threw the small plastic bag on to the desk. 'This might just dry up. And, by the way, it would help the image if you didn't come here dressed in jeans and sweatshirt. I think you'd look sensational in one of those tight-fitting all-in-one numbers. Some make-up wouldn't go amiss either.'

Jake waddled out of the room, stopped at the door and winked at her.

Alison took the little plastic bag, ripped it open and licked some of the powder. There followed another rummaging session through her handbag, but the syringe was not there.

'Damn it!'

The toilet was two doors along. She passed one of the other 'offices' on the way; she could hear pathetic chuckles and 'oohs' and 'aahs' coming from it. There were two cubicles and two washbasins in the spartan room. The cracked plaster and the graffiti were a fitting reflection of the 'office' - a squalid and greasy mess, trickles of rusty-coloured water oozing from cracked drainage pipes and the perpetual smell of piss.

She opened one of the cubicles and closed the door that did not have a lock. On pulling down her jeans and panties, she felt inside herself. The blisters were still there and that yellow, pus-like discharge had not gone away. Urinating was so painful, sharp spasms of pain shooting up inside her like alternating electric shocks. Of course there was no toilet paper, but she had a used handkerchief. That would have to do.

The wall mirror was cracked. It was like a glacial spider's web and it projected four eyes, sharply distorted lips, juxtaposed eyelashes, random polygons of ashen flesh. It seemed to reflect a contorted reality where senses and images were forever in disharmony. Seeing straight - what did that mean now? How did one go about doing it? What was a man? A woman? A child? What was the difference between sex and love? But getting on to the mundane, the paper round of life. Was there a difference in the smell between carbolic soap and Chanel Number 5? It didn't really matter when she was loaded.

She combed her hands through the crew cut. That, she reminded herself, was the result of a three-day bender last week. In fact it was the only event worth remembering. The other, which she would rather forget, had been ending up in a field just outside town, her dress stripped from her body and crusty flakes of blood caked to the insides of her thighs.

She patted her face with some water before tending the phone. Sitting at the desk, she yearned to get home, to wrap herself up in bed and fix.

The telephone buzzed.

'Hello,' she began, 'I'm Rosy. Who do I have the pleasure of talking with? Hmmm?'

'Yeah, hi, I'm Bob,' the voice began nervously. 'I needed to talk... to talk with someone. Are you... do you...'

'Hi, Bob, how are you, then? Are you lonely? I'm lonely too, Bobby. So take your time. I'm oh so easy to talk to, Bob. What do you want to talk about? Hmmm?'

'It's... it's... sex. I need sex, Rosy. Can... can... can I have sex with you?'

'Ah, Bob, dear Bob. We can have sex over the wire. I'd just love to make love to you over the telephone. Hahhhh. Now, if you'll just sit back. Get yourself comfortable and we'll come together, Bob. Hmmm.'

'Uh... I don't quite know how to...'

'Relax, Bob. Hmmm, I'm feeling so relaxed myself now. In fact, Bob, my hand is already way down inside my lacy, satin knickers, Bob. Oh, yes, it feels so good, Bob.'

And then the phone went dead. Yet another punter couldn't go the distance.

She stepped out on to the street and headed briskly towards the bus-stop. On the other side of the road, a pair of eyes followed the girl, the head steady on strong, broad shoulders. The head made a circular movement as if staving off stiffness in the neck. It slowly turned to keep the girl in sight. The breathing was deep with a pronounced wheeze. He made his way across the road and began tailing the girl at distance. *I just want you, baby. Maybe tonight, tomorrow night, next week. I can wait, baby. I've got your number in more ways than one. Soon, baby, very, very soon now. Perhaps in your place tonight, maybe in mine. Doesn't really matter. You've fucked me around long enough...*

The bus came as a welcome refuge from the prison cell of her work. Even such a simple procedure as getting on the bus, paying her fare and putting herself down on a seat was an achievement. Upstairs was smoky, and the rolling of the bus as it turned corners left her with a queasiness in the stomach.

In fact at one point the bus came to such an abrupt halt after having rounded a corner that her handbag tipped over on to the floor. She gazed anxiously around her, worried that someone might have noted the little plastic bag. Even though the bus was half-empty, such was the neurosis that seemed to follow her around like a shadow that the little package appeared to her as a two-pound bag of sugar.

Alison retrieved the contents of her handbag from the floor and began rolling another cigarette. The cigarette papers were damp, however, and she struggled to prise them apart. Finally overcoming that hurdle, she laid out the tobacco on the paper and began rolling it between shivering fingers. Tobacco strands peppered her lap, and more of the stuff seemed to be there than in the roll-up.

'Tickets, please. Tickets.' The inspector was at the top of the stairs. The roll-up looked more like a withered twig. Where the hell was her ticket? There followed another venture into the handbag. Why was the thing in such a bloody mess? The book of matches she put to one side.

'Tickets, please. Your tickets.' The voice was getting louder. There was a harsh, formal ring to it.

She instinctively put the roll-up in her mouth. There were only two matches left in the book. The first one broke. Striking the second one, it lit momentarily before the tip dropped off the end and landed on the floor.

'Shit!'

The ticket inspector was behind her. 'Tickets, please, sir.'

The voice asked, 'Ith Cambridge Thtreet the next thtop?'

Alison jumped to her feet, only to find her legs trembling like two sticks of quick-setting jelly.

'It's two stops down, sir.'

'No, no, no, no!' she screamed. 'Get away from me!'

Palpitations. The instant throbbing felt as though her heart might explode. Her arms, legs and head all shook visibly, like some old jalopy that was not firing on all cylinders. For a split second a wave of blackness passed over her sight. Unconsciousness was a heartbeat away. The insides of her gums and tongue felt as though they were coated with sandpaper.

The voice was directly behind her head. 'Thomething wrong, mith?'

'You have your ticket, madam?' the inspector asked.

Despite the bus's motion, she lunged past the ticket inspector, her head turned to the side, not wanting to see, to witness the sight of the pervert. She just had to get off the bus. Seeing nothing, wishing to forget the immediate hell she felt inside, she ran past the alarmed faces of the passengers on the upper deck and scrambled down the spiral staircase, to leap off the vehicle and come to a crashing halt against a wall.

'Thtrange woman, Inthpector!'

Alison triple-locked the door to her bedsit and leaned back against the door, gasping for breath. It was funny in the most ironic way that having used the phone day in, day out as part of her job, the very thing she needed more than ever right now was a bloody telephone. But she knew deep down inside that there was no way she could splash out on a mobile when she had a £150 a week smack habit to feed. Fuck mobile telephone contracts - her contracts might eventually turn out to be a matter of life and death.

Her eye caught sight of a buff-coloured envelope on the floor. It was from the clinic, Dr Mathieson, the specialist who had been treating her and who had carried out the tests. She picked it up and read the 'Private and Confidential' message stretched above the address window. Inside she knew the result would be one or the other, with not the remotest chance of anything in between. She put the envelope down on a nearby table.

She went through to the living room-cum-bedroom where, behind a lace net curtain, was her kitchenette. Jimi Hendrix stared down on her from a poster directly above the bed. On a bedside table sat a half-empty bottle of vodka, a plate, a spoon, a syringe and a lighter. She cast off her black velvet jerkin, which tumbled to the floor in a heap. Unscrewing the cap from the bottle, she guzzled down half of the vodka and winced. That seemed to steady her nerves. Then it was back to the handbag, fumbling for the powder, and eventually upending everything in the bag on the bed in her frustration in putting together the fix.

She tapped the white powder into the spoon and began heating the underside. Within moments it was liquid. Transferring that to the syringe, she pumped it to rid the syringe of any air. A minute jet of liquid spurted from the tip. Then she wrapped the narrow leather belt around her forearm. The veins hardly stood out, even though she increased the pressure of the tourniquet.

She slapped her forearm vigorously to the point where it turned red. Many of the previous pin-pricks had turned to blotches, reddish-blue lumps with creamy heads. The arm looked more like a medical school specimen than a limb belonging to a living member of the human race. She plunged the needle into a vein like aiming a dart at a dartboard, then depressed the plunger all the way down to the bottom.

Moments later, she laid her head against the pillow and closed her eyes. A spontaneous normality returned to her body, the muscles loosening, that vice-like band of tension across her forehead easing, leaving a cursory blissfulness. It was as if every single molecule in her being had come alive, freed from some organic prison. Then those sexual feelings returned, that inordinate, overwhelming drive for sex. It was an addiction that was curiously analogous to her heroin needs. Right now, as with so many times in the past, she would have fucked any man who walked into the room. Any man?

There was that letter by the front door. Her memory returned, reality setting in. She went to get the letter and lay down on the bed. It reminded her of the time when she had sat her 'O' levels, the impending trepidation of whether it was a pass or failure. But this was not exam results. This could be serious.

She thumbed the envelope open and withdrew the single sheet of paper.

HIV negative.

The sheer joy of relief overwhelmed her whole being as she slumped down on the floor and cried her eyes out.

'Hasn't Jake done anything about it?' Marie, her friend, asked.

'That sod? He couldn't give two continental fucks about me. Another drink?'

'Okay.'

Alison stepped over to the kitchenette and returned with the vodka bottle. Then she topped up their glasses; no juice, no ice, no water, just neat spirit.

Marie, like Alison, was 23 years old. They could have been identical twins, had it not been for Marie's brunette hair and sticky-out ears.

'Here,' Alison said, handing Marie her drink. 'Jake's one of those bastards who enjoy living off other people's misfortunes.'

'There's a lot of them about, Alison. But this has been going on for what, six months?'

'You know, I don't know who's worse, Jake or that bloody pervert. And there was me yesterday. I had a chance to look at him but somehow I couldn't bring myself to do it. And that thing he's got... what d'you call it?... a lisp.'

'A lisp, Alison?'

'Yeah. He's got a lisp. It's frightening, Marie. Yesterday when he called I felt like retching. I thought I'd throw up. It's too scary for words.'

'There must be something we can do,' Marie said.

'Like what? Call the cops? No, I don't think so. Jake's got me by the short and curlies on that score. No, I suspect I'll just go away into a little corner somewhere and try and die in peace.' She laughed. 'I've even thought about overdosing.'

'No way, Alison. That's not right. Look, I'll be here. Listen,' she said, changing the subject, 'there's a party on at the pub tomorrow night. What do you say? I've got some charlie back at my place. We could get loaded and get all dolled up and really go for it. Yeah?'

Alison raised her glass and smiled the widest of smiles. 'Okay. Let's do it.'

'And if that bastard calls you tomorrow, tell him to come along.'

'Right. You're on.'

The pub was small and smoky with tables snuggled into little nooks and crannies. There were so many people packed into such a tiny space that even the ancient oak ceiling rafters seemed to sweat. It was like a hard rock café, but the music here was house. Heads bobbed, bulging eyes stared into nothingness, permanent smiles were stretched across ashen faces. Everybody was on something.

Alison and Marie sat with two young men who earlier had tried to chat them up. But as Marie said, they were young, a couple of kids zonked out on god knows what. And there was that female who had stood at the end of the bar.

Alison was wearing a short black velvet skirt, fish-net stockings and underneath, a black lacy basque. She needed action, just as Marie had said earlier, the minute they walked into the place. The two of them had acknowledged the admiring glances. Who would it be tonight? There was some heroin back at her bedsit, she said to herself, but that was for her when she got home, preferably with a guy who knew how to use it.

'Look, Marie, I'll have to go to the toilet.' She drained her glass. 'I'll have another vodka, by the way.'

'All right. Oh, have you got any condoms?' Marie asked with a smile.

'Maybe three, four.'

'Just to be on the safe side, you know.'

'But of course. Good thinking, gal!'

Alison got to her feet and momentarily adjusted her skirt down the way. Squeezing her way through countless sweaty bodies, she reminded herself that she was HIV negative and that because of the circles she moved in, a condom was always a safety net against possible disease and death.

There were two girls waiting on the cubicles when she arrived, so she took the opportunity to do her lips. More girls arrived. She eventually got into one of the cubicles and locked the door. It was second from the end one, the latter being next to the wall of the toilet. As she slid her skirt down, a fingernail caught the top of a stocking and tore it slightly. 'Damn, these cost six bloody quid!' She began to sort that out.

What are you doing next door my thweet? It would be tho eathy to pop my head over the top. Or maybe look at you from the underthide. You didn't thee me at the bar. I thaw you though. Your girlfriend thaw me but thee didn't know who I wath. Hee, hee, hee...

Alison flushed the toilet, stepped out and inspected herself in the mirror. The door to the adjoining toilet opened and a woman stood beside her. Their eyes met in the mirror. The woman smiled at Alison as she commenced washing her hands. There was a bit of commotion as three girls, pissed out of their minds, entered. They were cursing and swearing, shrieking with laughter at the tops of their voices. One of them bumped into Alison, who in turn knocked into the woman next to her.

'Oh, I'm sorry, I think you'll have to excuse them. They're a bit drunk,' Alison said.

The woman looked Alison straight in the eye. 'Don't worry my dear.'

Alison could only stare. If there was such a thing as vibrations that emanated from people, she knew exactly what that meant. The bedlam being created by the girls immediately faded out, like a sound track on a film. It was as if they were the only two human beings alive. No words were spoken, only mental images flowing between them through the ether. Hers were fabricated from fear, whilst the stranger's issued from some kind of libidinous derangement.

Alison, her eyes staring, unwavering, asked, 'It's you, isn't it?'

He ran a nicotine-stained tongue slowly along his glossy, crimson lips. 'Yeth.'

It was probably because she was loaded that she found herself able to out-stare this misfit. High noon in the toilet, she thought, and, suddenly, she was not afraid any more. After all, he was only a human being. All those wretched calls began to fall into place. This was a pitiful creature in front of her with a misplaced mind in search of a convalescent home.

She began to laugh at him, to chuckle at his painted face, the sloppy blouse and the knee-length pleated skirt and that blonde curly wig, the type of thing that would attract belly laughs from a circus audience. The maniac's head began to twitch from side to side, eyes rolling around in their sockets, lips puckered.

Suddenly the racket and commotion faded up once more. One of the girls had fallen over and her two pals were making brave attempts to get her to her feet.

'Okay then,' Alison began loudly, in a more rigorous tone, 'I am Rosy and I am here to please you. Now what do you really want? Hmmm?'

He was tongue-tied for an instant, even began blushing. 'I... I don't know.' The words were frail and broken. 'Thomehow you are different, theeing you like this. I feel embarathed now.'

'Oh, come on, my sweet, as you would say. Do you want to fuck me? Because that's what you keep telling me. Look,' she said, pulling her skirt all the way up over her thighs. Some of the girls turned to look at Alison, which brought on more fits of laughter, then whistles, jeering, lewd asides. 'There now. How's that?'

Next it was her top that she opened. She took out one of her breasts. 'Right, my sweetie, this is a tit - a real tit. It's a 34D. Would you like to see the other? Hmmm?'

There was a dubiety about this clown's glance, an uncertainty of emotion, and then a single tear dangled from a crudely-painted eyelash. His conscience, or what was left of it, might implode any minute now.

'Pleathe, I'm... I'm a lonely man. I needed thomeone to talk to. I... I need to go now. I'm thorry for causing you any...'

Before he could say any more Alison turned to the rest of the girls. Now she was in control. Now she had this pervert exactly where she wanted him.

'Girls. See this queen we've got here. This one makes erotic telephone calls. He's forever phoning me, tormenting me, telling me what he wants to do to me. He's always going on about wanting into my knickers. Then about all the positions he'd take me in. Well, girls, he's got his chance now, hasn't he?'

One of the girls yelled, 'Get 'em off!' Another, 'Let's strip him!' And another, 'Yeah, let's do it!'

They all attacked him en masse. Off came the wig. Then Alison ripped the blouse all the way down the middle. He fell to the floor, the girls tearing away at the skirt like a herd of wild boar. What had started off as heady bedlam in the bog quickly slid into rampant farce. His clothes were being ripped off as a flock of vultures would pick away at a bloody carcass. The girls were yelling and howling to get at his underpants, which turned out to be the minutest of frilly laces in pink. Alison then instructed them to pin him to the floor. His make-up by now was smudged and smeared, the tears having washed away the mascara, leaving two big black eyes. He was pleading with Alison to stop, at which point she did. She stood over her naked prey with arms akimbo, domineering.

'Now, my sweet,' she said, 'you're gonna get what you always wanted.'

'No, pleathe, no. I beg you, pleathe.'

She slid her skirt all the way down until it dropped on the floor. Stepping out of it, she began to slowly slide her knickers off, all the time her eyes fixed on his. The girls started chanting, urging Alison to get on with it, to rape the bastard. Then she tossed the knickers on his face.

'If I remember right, you always wanted oral sex. Right?'

He was shaking his head from side to side. 'No, Rothy, for Godth thake. Pleathe.'

'But you kept telling me that over the phone, fuck-face!'

He began to whimper like a little, innocent baby. The pleas were getting not to make sense; they were just a mixture of impeded vowel sounds and garbled consonants.

Alison got down and straddled his face. 'Right, you bastard, do it. Do it! Do it!' she screamed.

And then suddenly: 'Alison, what the hell are you doing?' Marie shouted.

All the girls' heads turned toward the toilet door. Marie entered and pushed her way to the front.

Alison turned to her friend. 'This,' she said upon getting to her feet, 'is the mysterious caller. Take a good look at him, Marie. This is him.'

'But what are you doing?' she asked again. 'What's this all about?'

'Oh, I'm just giving this asshole the chance to realise all his wonderful fantasies. All the shit I've had to put up with for all these months.'

'Come on, Alison, let's go. Leave it at that.'

Alison removed a shoe, the heel of which measured four inches, turned to the man and straddled him once more. He was still whimpering like a child. 'Right now I could blind you with this. I won't, but let me tell you something, if you ever phone me again, I'll track you down, come hell or high water, just like you did to me. And what's more, the next time it'll be for real. And this little thing here,' she said, fiddling his penis with the stiletto heel, 'will be pulled out with the roots and stuffed right down your throat. Get it?'

His head shook, a foamy spittle edging its way down the side of a mouth agape with fear.

Marie grabbed Alison's arm. 'Look, Marie, get dressed and let's get out of here before the bouncers arrive. You could get arrested.'

'Me? Arrested? It's that shit there that needs arresting. Just look at him.'

'Okay, Alison, point taken. Now, come on.'

Alison turned to him for the last time. 'There's just one remaining piece of business. What's your name?'

'Name? Uh, eh, ith... ith Garry. Garry Watling,' he replied.

'Right. And the address?'

'Addreth?' he said, still twittering and twitching.

'Yes,' she shouted, 'your fucking address!'

'Okay, okay. Fifty... fifty-nine, Wood Park... Terrace.'

'Good,' she replied. Turning to Marie and pulling up her skirt, she ended, 'I've got all I need now.'

Alison was back manning the telephone on Monday

afternoon. She took Jake's advise of the previous week and got herself dressed up 'to look the part' as he wanted. Her dress sense reflected a new found confidence that resulted in a resolution to kick her heroin addiction for good. In fact she had been back to the doctor in the morning and commenced a programme of recovery. It would not be easy, but she reckoned she now had the will to win. Jake had taken the day off and, over a cup of coffee, she took the telephone directory.

'Now let's see,' she said browsing through the Ws. 'Watling? Interesting.' There were two Watlings in the book. G. Watling, 59, Wood Park Terrace. The other...

'Watling and Kruger Solicitors,' she mumbled out aloud. 'It gets more interesting by the minute.'

She underlined the Wood Park Terrace address and keyed in the number. It rang.

'One-seven-six-five-two-two.' The female voice sounded almost noble and educated.

'Yes, this is Miss Cathy Page speaking. Is Mr Watling in please?'

'No, I'm afraid he's at the office. Can I take a message?'

'Sorry to bother you and that but he is Garry Watling, the solicitor? It's just that I need some legal advice.'

'Well, Miss Page, if you'd like to phone him at the office, I'm sure he'll be able to accommodate you. Do you need the number?'

'No, I'll get it from Yellow Pages. Thanks.'

'Okay, bye.'

'Bye, bye, now.'

She rubbed her hands together and immediately keyed in the office number and waited. It seemed to ring for ages. Then.

'Good afternoon, Watling and Kruger, can I help you?'

'Yes, I'd like to speak with Mr Watling if I may.'

'Hold the line, please.'

Then a click, followed by an irritating, chiming jingle rendition of *Morning Has Broken*. This persisted for half a minute and then an abrupt click. 'Garry Watling, can I help you?'

She put on that sultry, inviting cadence and laid it on heavier than ever. 'Maybe,' she said.

'Who ith thith?' he asked.

She paused for a long moment breathing very gently into the receiver. 'You don't recognise my voice, Garry? My sweetness?'

'Look, I think you have the wrong number,' he replied hesitantly.

'Oh no, Garry, I've got your number all right. You see I'm Rosy and I'm here to please you, for you to do with me as you please. Hmmm?'

There was a moment's silence. 'Listen, I don't want to talk to you. Now bugger off!'

'Bugger off? Oh, that's awful rude of you, Garry. Yes, I'm going to bugger off right now. And you know what, Garry? My next call will be to your wife. By the way, Garry, it was hellish knowing you.'

She slammed down the receiver.

Models of Excellence

It was the happiest day in Sean Brightwell's life. The handsome, fair-haired stockbroker had just taken delivery of his Ferrari Testarossa - red, of course. And at the age of twenty-eight, he reckoned he'd finally arrived.

The long, red wedge sat majestically in the driveway of his £500,000 detached villa on the outskirts of St Albans, just off the M25 motorway. The bright red paintwork shone in the midday sun and the alloy wheels glistening, the tinted windows reflecting the willow trees to one side of the driveway.

He stood back and admired the machine. Yes, he thought, all the hassles, all the late nights over the past two years slaving over endless clients' portfolios in the City, had come to this supreme moment. With a brand new duster in hand, he lovingly wiped over the wing mirrors and windows with all the care and attention that an Oscar winner would give to the little golden statuette.

He opened the driver's door and eased himself into the cockpit. The door shut with a reassuring click. The smell of the tan hide was delicious. And then a stupid thought entered his mind. How many cattle had contributed their skins to this beautiful upholstery? Crazy, he thought to himself, dismissing the thought.

And the sound system. The six speaker Technics stereo was a personal aberration on his part, and at 300 watts, it would be commensurate with the mammoth 520 brake horsepower lodged in the engine bay behind him.

He got out of the car, turning to cast an admiring glance over those sleek Pininfarina lines, and returned to the house. As it was Sunday and he wouldn't be seeing Constance till later, he decided he would take the car down to his local, the Bohemian. The Ferrari roared into life upon starting and then loosened itself off into a rumble. He reversed the car out of the drive and sped away down the road, a cloud of dust momentarily obscuring the enormous rear end.

Within minutes, he was approaching the Bohemian, a quaint Tudor building with patterned brickwork and drip-moulded and leaded lozenge windows. The large patio accommodated rickety tables and chairs around which sat the local 'set', mostly yuppie types, sipping on German bottled beers and trying to look intellectual. Whatever conversation they were presently engaged in came to an abrupt halt when Sean steered the Ferrari into the car park. Heads turned, beers were placed back onto the tables and mouths fell agape. The ladies lifted the sunglasses off their noses, not so much admiring the car as establishing who was in the driver's seat. Several young kids playing on the pavement nearby immediately surrounded the car.

Sean turned off the ignition, climbed out and locked the door. He picked out the oldest looking of the kids and handed him two one-pound coins.

'Make sure nobody, and I mean nobody, lays even a fingernail on this car. All right?'

The youngster quickly pocketed the money. 'Yes, sir!'

Sean noticed two of his friends, Greg and Larry, sitting ogling the car. He went over and sat down beside them.

Greg said, 'So you finally got it, I see.'

'Yep,' Sean replied, turning to look at the car. 'She's quite beautiful.'

'Bloody poser,' Larry said jokingly.

'I suppose I'll have to get used to people saying that. Boring really.'

'Has Constance seen it yet, Sean?' Greg asked.

'Hang on, folks.' He motioned to the waitress. 'Oh, Jenny, bring us three beers, will you? Right, where was I. Oh, yeah, Constance. No, she's not seen it - yet.'

'Well she's going to love it,' Greg said. 'You know what women are like when it comes to cars. Hell, you could pick up any girl driving that. Lucky bastard!'

'Well I ain't picking up any girls, Greg, right?'

'Right.'

The drinks arrived. Jenny had retained a shapely body, but her face didn't quite match up to her legs. She placed their drinks on the table. She cast an amorous glance at

Brightwell before focusing her attention on the car. 'Must have set you back a bit, Sean.'

'If you've got it, flaunt it, Jenny. Just like you do with that lovely round bottom of yours,' Sean replied.

She stared away. 'That'll be eleven pounds.' Sean handed her the money and Jenny left.

'Anyway, how much did she set you back?' Larry asked.

Sean sipped on the bottle. 'One hundred and nine grand.'

'More money than sense if you ask me,' Larry said. 'Ninety-eight grand on a car? Crazy, Sean, bloody crazy.'

'You drive a Rover, Larry, right?'

'Right.'

'And it gets you from the proverbial A to B, right?

'Right.'

'Well, Larry, the Ferrari gets me from A to B as well. But it gets me there in style. That's the difference.'

'Still think you're crazy.'

'So you're seeing Constance later, Sean?' Greg asked.

'Yeah, around six.' He took another mouthful from the bottle and checked his watch. 'In fact I should be going. See you lot later.'

As Sean strolled back to the car, he was conscious of something like thirty pairs of eyes following him. The kids were still looking into the windows of the car, watched over eagerly by the oldest kid.

'Thanks, son.'

The kid asked, 'Is that a real Ferrari, mister?'

'It sure is, son. You too can own one of these when you're older. So you stick in at school. Okay?'

'I will, mister, I will.'

Sean got into the car and switched on the ignition. This time he pressed the accelerator pedal hard onto the floor. The engine screamed behind him, and the kids on the pavement were suddenly stunned by the raw power of the red beast. For their amusement, he held the handbrake to the last minute before letting out the clutch. Burning rubber smoked on the tarmacadam as the Ferrari flew down past the pub, heads turning, sunglasses raised, conversation stopped.

She was dressed in a red skin-tight skirt which was cut way above the knee. Above that she wore a white silk blouse and a black matador-style jacket. Her auburn hair was lifted up into a bun, a string of pearls looped around her delicate neck. Those were a twenty-third birthday present given to her by Sean last year. The make-up was quite lavishly but tastefully applied on this warm, balmy evening.

She stepped out of the taxi, clutching a miniature handbag. There was no car in the driveway, but she noticed the kitchen light was on. The door was open, so she let herself in.

'Sean? Sean? Are you there?'

Sean entered the kitchen from the living room with two glasses of white wine. He handed her one. 'You look absolutely stunning, darling.' He kissed her. 'Yes, stunning, just like my new...'

'Ferrari?' she continued excitedly. 'Where is it? I've just got to see this new toy of yours.'

'Okay.'

He took her by the hand and led her to the garage. The door lifted up, and once inside the garage he flicked on the light. The fluorescent lamp bathed the car with a showroom aura. It looked more spectacular than ever.

'Sean,' Constance said almost with bated breath, 'it's... it's... immaculate. Truly immaculate!'

'Yeah, I know. Hang on.'

Sean got into the car, reversed it on to the driveway and switched off the ignition.

'Well then?' he asked proudly.

'Oh, Sean, what can I say? Are we taking it for a spin tonight?' she asked, walking round the machine and dragging a fingertip delicately over the gleaming paintwork.

'Only if you're good to me,' he replied. 'Now stay there, don't move.'

He stepped into the house and arrived back several minutes later. He set a digital camera up on a wall of the driveway and positioned Constance at the front of the car. Then he set the automatic timer on the camera and quickly posed alongside his girlfriend. Within a moment he, Constance and the Ferrari were recorded for posterity on a humble microchip.

'Right. I'll get rid of this contraption and maybe you can powder your nose, or whatever girls do, then it's off down to the Bohemian.'

'Super, Sean. Super.'

Sean got into the driver's seat whilst Constance struggled inelegantly in arranging herself in the passenger's. He couldn't help notice her little skirt ride up the full length of her legs. He smacked his lips at the gorgeous sight and she stuck her tongue out at him. And then she banged the door shut.

'Hey! Easy, easy. This isn't your Golf, Constance. Yeah?' he said acidly.

'Sorry, sorry.' She glared at him.

The Bohemian was mobbed: all the old faces, the posers, the pseudo-intellectuals, the piss artists, they were all there. As in the afternoon, heads turned, drinks were placed on tables and the psychobabble tailed off to a mumble. The Ferrari had arrived.

Constance took it all in her stride. She had been one of the biggest show-offs in town for ages. Being a model helped, of course, legs up to her armpits and a face that would grace any front cover of *Vogue* magazine, any year, any decade.

She pulled her skirt down to a respectable level with her fingertips and took Sean's arm as they approached the cluster of tables outside the pub. They acknowledged their friends, but decided to sit down at an empty table close to the bar entrance. Sean ordered a half-bottle of red wine and a Perrier water.

Constance said, 'So it's back to work tomorrow, Sean. Oh, how I just hate Mondays.'

'Honestly?'

'Oh! I see you've changed your tune.'

'Mondays will never be the same again, my sweet. Not with that car to come home to every night. It's given me a new perspective on life.'

'You mean you're not driving it to work?'

Sean laughed. 'Drive the Testarossa to work? Into the City? Absolutely not. Never. Besides, that five-litre engine would struggle to return 12 miles to the gallon in city traffic. No, I'll take the train as usual. And I'll tell you something else,' he said glancing lovingly over at the car, 'that car won't even be driven in rain.'

'Oh, come on, Sean. Aren't you taking this a bit far? At the end of the day it's only a blinking car.'

'It? It, my sweet, is a her, a she.'

Constance let out a loud snigger just as their drinks arrived. She had the wine whilst Sean settled for the Perrier. There followed a light meal of lemon sole and ice-cream and in between there transpired a sort of tennis match: she forcing the conversation about her career and he interjecting enthusiastically about the great, red wedge. And on it went.

They were ready to go.

'So,' Sean ended, 'coffee at my place or yours?'

'I think not tonight, Sean. I'm not feeling that great now.' She belched. 'I'm sorry. I think that fish didn't agree with me.'

'What?' he asked. 'What's up?'

'Not tonight, darling. As I said, that fish has given me a sore stomach. Let's go.'

'Fair enough,' he said forcefully. 'Anything you say.'

Sean paid the bill and stepped away from the table, leaving the girl to follow him at a distance. She was at the door of the car.

'There was no need for that, Sean,' she said.

He opened the driver's door. 'For what, huh?'

'Forget it.'

'I'll drop you off.'

Sean was sitting in the office scanning the VDU for foreign currency figures coming in overnight from Hong Kong. They were very encouraging. He made some calculations and entered them into a ledger. The office itself was an open-plan affair accommodating some fifty or so dealers and even at this very early hour in the morning, the phones rang, keyboards clicked and deals were being shouted by telephone from one desk to another. It was all very hectic.

One of Sean's colleagues, Ronnie, arrived with the coffees.

'Ah,' said Sean, 'you're a lifesaver. Just what the doctor ordered.'

Ronnie sat down. 'So how's the Ferrari, Sean?'

'Brilliant. Yeah, great.'

'And Constance?'

'Loves it.' He laughed. 'She reckons I go on about it too much though.'

'But that's your prerogative, is it not?'

'Try telling her that. Anyway, how's the Porsche?'

'Okay, I suppose. But it's got an oil leak. Discovered it last night.'

'Oh dear.'

'Yeah, I know. Christ knows how much that's gonna set me back,' Ronnie said disconsolately.

'Well, Ronnie, if you own these exotic cars and all that, you've got to be prepared to come up with the readies. Never mind, you can afford it.

'Well, I'll put it in for a check tomorrow, then we'll take it from there.'

Sean's phone bleeped, at which point Ronnie returned to his desk. Sean lifted the receiver. 'Sean Brightwell,' he stated. 'Constance, how are you? Yeah, I'm fine... no, not at the moment. Lunch? OK, half one. Right, see you there.'

He placed down the receiver and took out his wallet from his jacket pocket. Inside was the digital photograph he had printed out of him and Constance posing in front of the Ferrari. He smiled and sank deeper into his chair. A beautiful woman and an equally beautiful car - Paradise!

They were dining on salmon sandwiches in *Harpers*, a fashionable wine bar in the City, much frequented by high flyers in the business world. Sean topped up her glass with the red wine. He had earlier presented her with an enlarged, framed photograph of the two of them posing with the Ferrari.

'As I was saying,' Constance said, 'if all goes well, the next shoot will be in the south of France.'

'South of France?' Sean asked curiously.

'Monaco, to be exact. Oh, it's so romantic, Sean, the Cote d'Azur, clear blue skies, yachts, great shopping and the food. Wow!'

'And the men?' he asked as an afterthought.

'What about the men?'

'Well you know what they say about the French. Ooh la la, and all that.'

'Sean - darling. You needn't worry about me and men. You should know that by now. Look, I love you,' she ended, taking his hand in hers.

'Yeah, I know, and I love you too,' Sean replied. 'Well, with you being away, I suppose I'll have my Ferrari to play with.'

She shrugged her shoulders and glowered at him. 'See? There you go again.' She let go of his hand.

'What?'

'The car. Ever since you bought it, it's been the car, the car and nothing else but the car. It does get tiresome, Sean. There's more to life than a blinking car, you know.'

'Oh yeah? Well there's more to life than cavorting about semi-naked and letting horny assholes who call themselves photographers cajole you into all those strange positions you get into. Shit, they probably get great sexual pleasure from it. Huh?' he ended angrily.

Several people from adjoining tables couldn't help staring in their direction. She paused and looked at him straight in the eye. 'Quite finished?'

Sean gulped down some more wine. He said pensively, I'm sorry, Constance. I didn't mean to say that. Will you forgive me?'

'Look, I must be going. I have a very important meeting with one of those horny assholes, as you put it, in twenty minutes' time.'

Constance wiped her mouth with a serviette and finished her wine. Sean smiled awkwardly and asked, 'Is it still on for the party tomorrow night?'

'I think so.'

'Will I pick you up then, or what?'

'No, Sean, I'll drive myself to the party in my little, simple Golf GTi.' She was on her feet. 'All of a sudden your superstud of a car doesn't turn me on any more.'

She stomped out of the bar.

'Bastards,' Sean whispered to himself.

Sean took the rest of the day off. To hell with the office. They can do without me for an afternoon. Then there was Constance. Why were things changing between them all of a sudden? The car - that's what it was. He knew it all right; didn't make any bones about it. But it was that beautiful piece of Italian engineering sitting outside on the driveway. Of course he knew it. But he loved the car, and as Ronnie had said earlier that morning, it was his prerogative to talk about it. Hell, everybody he knew asked him about it: the engine size, its speed, wheelbase, tyres, transmission, wheels, power.

He sat behind the wheel of the great machine and donned his black suede driving gloves. He looked into the rear view mirror and touched up his hair. Yes, he thought, cars don't talk back to you. Switching on the ignition, he revved the 12 cylinders until they were screaming for mercy, the absolute power exhilarating: man and machine, what a combination, almost sexual in makeup and the sheer class of the Prancing Horse.

'Right baby,' he said out aloud, 'let's see what you're really made of.'

It was mid-afternoon when he pulled off the M1 and joined the M25 motorway heading eastwards. Between St Albans and the M25 he had been tailed by somebody in a souped-up Honda Accord. This was something he would have to get used to: sightseers on the motorway, boy-racers playing futile games. Well, it was only natural. It wasn't every day that one comes across a Ferrari on the roads - and a classic red Testarossa at that.

The M25 was thankfully quite lean on traffic and, after three miles, there were no signs of police patrol cars. He slipped the Ferrari into the fast lane and, at 85 miles per hour, the car seemed to be just warming up. Passing traffic on the middle lane, it was a case of heads turning, fingers pointing. Up to 95 now; it was smooth and effortless, although the rock hard suspension, so delicate in its geometry, juddered on the slightest of bumps on the tarmacadam. But the well-engineered aerodynamics of the vehicle, and the vast bulk of rubber acting like magnets between ground and machine, ensured that it held fast in a straight line.

One hundred miles per hour: the ton. Cars up ahead began to rush towards him, but his foot was pushing ever downwards in a kind of battle of nerves between mind and power. Now he felt he knew what it must be like to be behind the wheel of a Formula One car approaching the finishing straight at Silverstone. The cars up ahead pulled into the middle lane as he approached 110. Streams of perspiration began to trickle down his temples as he glanced at the speedometer, his hands firmly clamped to the Momo steering wheel. The needle was fast approaching 130. The traffic in the middle lane was now flashing by him and the absolute exuberance, the high, the intoxicating G-forces that had him pinned against the seat.

One hundred and fifty miles per hour, and all of a sudden his radar scanner bleeped. Shit, he thought. And up ahead a police patrol car parked on the hard shoulder. Had it broken down?

His foot hit the brake pedal and there was a screech of rubber as the ventilated disc brakes did the business. He was then down to a respectable 100 miles per hour and looking in his rear view mirror, he saw the patrol car pulling off the hard shoulder and making tracks onto the middle lane. Sean, with a sudden burst of speed, pulled into the middle lane, dodging in and out of traffic, moved over onto the slow lane and exited the M25 at junction 25, the A10 to Hertford. The police car never stood a chance.

Sean was back home within the hour, having lost the law somewhere between Hertford and Hatfield. Now he knew what the Ferrari was capable of, but he figured he'd take the car to a German autobahn the next time.

The party was in full swing, the occasion being that of Frank Jennings' wife's fiftieth birthday. Frank was Sean's boss in the City. The large Edwardian country house was packed, mainly with company staff, City businessmen and personal friends of Frank. Frank was one of those jolly types, slightly overweight and balding, and he had an atrocious taste in braces and ties. The night had reached that point in any party where settees and chairs are put to one side and the dancing starts. It was getting close to midnight and with the raucous music and the laughter, everybody was having a ball.

Frank noticed Constance by the large fireplace. 'Constance, how are you?' he said, approaching her. They pecked each other on both cheeks.

'Oh, Frank, don't you know that's the third time you've asked me that tonight?'

'Silly billy. If only I was thirty years younger,' he said.

'Frank, that's the third time you've asked me that as well.' She drained her glass. 'However, you could be a proper darling and get me another gin and tonic.'

'For you, princess, any time. Let me.'

Frank took her glass and walked away towards the bar. She noted Sean talking to a girl. The girl in question was an old flame of Sean's, although she had since married. But they were laughing flippantly and there was a mischievousness about the way she regarded him.

Then Frank returned, momentarily distracting her from her thoughts.

'There, Constance, get that down you. It'll do you a power of good.'

Constance took the glass. She was still bobbing and weaving her head to get a glimpse of Sean and the woman. The gin and tonic went down in one.

'I'll have another, Frank - this time a large one.'

Frank took her glass and gave her a quizzical look. 'But of course.'

An hour later everybody was on the floor amid dancing, laughter, screams and squeals; the very floor was shaking as if there was a stampede in the offing. Constance waited until Sean had finished dancing with the girl and went, or rather staggered, over to him. She leered at the girl. 'You, lady, can fuck off now. Sean's my man.'

Sean turned to the girl. 'I'm sorry, Angela, I think Constance has had too much to drink.'

'Too much to drink, huh? I haven't even started yet.'

Angela didn't know where to look. 'There's my Derek over there. I think he wants to dance.' She ignored Constance completely. 'See you about, Sean.'

Sean grabbed Constance by the arm. 'What the hell are you playing at?'

'You've ignored me all night long. Well, haven't you?'

'Look, I don't want to make a scene, Constance. It just so happens that Angela's husband is working on some deals that I happen to be interested in. And that's all there is to it. D'you understand?'

She was swaying slightly and Sean held her arm tighter in an attempt to prevent her from falling over.

'I know what she's interested in, Sean. It's you. Ever since you broke up with her she's never hidden the fact that she'd like to bed you again. Is that not right, Sean?'

'You're drunk, Constance,' he said coldly.

The she gabbled louder, 'Oh I'm drunk, am I? Well that's great, because now you'll be able to fuck me without going through all the petty foreplay stuff you usually indulge in. Right, Mr Ferrari Man?'

'Look, Constance, keep your voice down or you're going to get very embarrassing.'

She sniggered and snorted, still swaying. 'Oh, I couldn't embarrass a big Ferrari man, could I?' Her voice changed into a more rebellious tone. 'A man who loves his fucking car more than me. Eh, Mr Ferrari Man?'

Sean nervously scratched his head. 'Constance, I think you should go home, all right? It's because I love you that I don't want you making a damned fool of yourself.'

All of a sudden the music tapered out and somebody checked through a pile of CDs for another sound. That was her cue.

'Did you hear that, everyone?' she shouted at the top of her voice. 'Sean Brightwell says he loves me.' All heads turned towards them. Laughter died down. There was absolute silence. 'This man, whom I love, bought a Ferrari something-or-other a couple of months ago. He loves it, adores it, treats it like another woman. Do you know what it's like loving a man like this? No? Then I'll tell you. It stinks!' She turned to Sean, tears streaming down her face. 'So Mr Ferrari, you can take your superstud of a car and stick it right up your asshole, because I'm off.'

Before Sean could do anything, Constance was running out of the house. The party-goers stared in amazement, Frank Jennings gazed on in bewilderment whilst Sean ran after her. As he reached the outside door, Constance was already behind the wheel of the Golf and speeding away down the drive towards the country road. Sean wasted no time in getting into the Ferrari and within minutes was trailing her some thirty yards behind. It was pitch black up ahead and the road twisted and turned. The Golf, however, was not tracking the bends in the road but swaying all over the place, skidding to one side then the other. Looking at his own speedo, he was doing 70 miles per hour, and all of a sudden fear gripped his throat. What to do? If he tried passing her she might crash into him, into his Ferrari. She might be killed. He might be killed. And to make things worse, he was not sure of this particular road, not aware of what lay up ahead.

He was doing 90 miles per hour when he noted her gesticulating at him. The Golf continued to sway all over the road. She was surely going to kill herself. He decided on a passing manoeuvre, but she pulled over to block him. Then he steered the Ferrari into the inside, but such was the sheer width of the Ferrari that overtaking was well-nigh impossible. He began flashing his full beams, tooting his horn, anything to get her to stop this madness. But to no avail. Tiny rivulets of sweat were streaming down both temples.

Now they were on a long straight stretch, and he decided on a final passing shot. With an instantaneous burst of acceleration he pulled up beside her, the two cars inches between them, approaching 100 miles an hour. He roared past her and quickly steered the Ferrari in front. In the same instant the Golf swayed perilously close to the side of the road and hit a huge pothole. The car flew up end over end and smashed into a tree with an enormous crash. The Golf burst into flames.

Sean climbed out of the Ferrari and dashed back along the darkened road, his heart in his mouth. On the grass beside the wreckage of the Golf, Constance lay motionless. Sean knelt down, frantically examining her. She had clearly crashed through the windscreen; her throat had been slashed by a shard of glass.

Sean lay beside her, weeping and whimpering. Why had it come to this? The conflagration of the burnt wreckage and nearby trees prompted him to drag her from the immediate area and put her down in a more comfortable spot. He held her in his arms, cuddling her like a baby, constantly repeating to himself why, why, why?

Then he looked back at the Ferrari, which was standing as majestically next to this scene of death as it did in the peaceful surroundings of his driveway. All the hype, all the prestige, the one-upmanship that went with owning something that most people just dream about had led to this unspeakable tragedy. It stank. It was bullshit. He cried out aloud, almost demented at what had happened. He laid her down gently and staggered towards the burning wreckage. From inside his wallet he withdrew the photograph which had meant so much to them both. Several feet away was a flaming branch. He lifted it, walked up to the dead body and paused.

'This is for you, Constance,' he murmured.

Breathless, he staggered up to the Ferrari and tossed

the picture onto the driver's seat. Then he opened the petrol cap, stuffed the burning branch inside and quickly stood back as the car exploded into a ball of fire.

What the Eye Doesn't See

The scorching sun glistened vibrantly off the serene current of the river, as time itself was carried along with the water to that other eternity called the ocean. Molecules, billions, trillions of them, particles of minuteness welded together by a phenomenon called electricity. Light, movement, space, time, it was all here, the sum total of the ageing universe right in front of my eyes. It was as if the river was trying to tell me something which, like myself, would undergo creation and destruction. Of course, I had taught these things for twenty-five years at the university, asking the questions, drawing up the equations and then demonstrating the solutions. Mathematics, man's great invention, could prove everything. And then I thought that if God created all this then he was sure one hell of a mathematician.

But it was the time. And it was the butterfly. The

butterfly skimmed across the river and alighted on a nearby reed. The arrival of the insect momentarily distracted me from my thoughts. What had the butterfly seen when it had crossed the river? Had it seen the molecules, the atoms, the weak and strong nuclear forces, the chaos represented by quantum mechanics? Of course not, but then I was interpreting things from the human angle, from the logical deduction which was a condition of human growth: education. It was funny, though, because I recalled what a biology teacher told me at high school, how to distinguish between a moth and a butterfly. The moth on landing sits with its wings spread out, whilst the butterfly brings its wings together. Did it really matter to the butterfly that a moth arranges its wings differently?

Sitting there quite happily, fascinated by the insect, my mind reverted to the water. This particular river originated some three hundred feet up on an adjacent hill. Depending on the rainfall, which was quite steady in this part of the world, the river would rush by this point at varying speeds on its downward search for the sea. How many molecules flowing down this river had at one time or another been here before, I wondered? I supposed the odds on that one were quite remote, but possible just the same. After all, once out to sea it would only take the westerly winds and a mixture of high and low weather fronts for a particular molecule to end up flowing back down the river again.

The butterfly seemed to be looking at me as I was looking at it. I leant further towards it for a closer look. The creature was about two inches wide, with spindly legs and glowing orange circles on its wings. Its antennae continually probed the air, as if searching for information. I could not help but wonder if its brain retained any vestiges of memory of its development from a caterpillar. My logic told me absolutely not. Never - no way. There I was again, though, interpreting a genuine possibility in the negative. That was the problem. When I took a class on quantum mechanics or Newton's theories of universal gravitation, I was at home, knowing that at the end of the day mathematics would come to my rescue. I could demonstrate Einstein's theories of relativity, explain the wave-particle phenomena of light, use Riemannian geometry and explain quantum fields. But I couldn't understand what was going on in that little insect's brain.

Did it really matter? If I knew the answer to that question, I would surely be in possession of the Truth.

Conditioning. That was the word that sprang to mind. All my life I had been conditioned, accustomed to habits, protocol and predetermination. Rules, laws, routines and systems had been shoved down my throat since the day I was born. Like everybody else, I grew up developing inventories of common sense behaviour, arranging, sorting and pigeonholing everything into nice neat bundles. Maybe it was because I blossomed in academia and encouraged by my parents and friends to aspire to that highest of all goals: a professorship. But it had all led to this, sitting by the water's edge, still asking questions and still as ignorant as ever.

The butterfly fluttered to another reed and sat there, its wings twitching, its antennae constantly exploring space.

What captivating beauty, I thought. The pastel hues of its wings, its singularly wonderful symmetry. This was real life.

I leant a little forward again and extended my hand to try and catch it, but it instantly flew several yards away and came to rest on another reed. Such awesome simplicity, I was thinking, but just then, in a moment of sheer destiny, it was gone, swooped up in the beak of a chaffinch. Cruelty, I said, but then the bird wouldn't have thought so. The bird had to live, and at this time of the year it might be feeding its young. Possibly the bird might end up as supper for a rabbit and the rabbit might be served up as Sunday dinner in some nearby farmhouse.

I had been sitting down by the river for an hour now and was becoming exceedingly irked by this carousel of contemplation. It was as if I had no control over it, like a train of thoughts passing through the stations of inference with no terminal in sight. The butterfly had come as a thought and left as a thought, as if its arrival and departure had never existed outside my head. This was leading me to utter despair, a feeling of loathing, a belief that nothing mattered any more. How was I to return home, to my wife and kids, to the *real* world, because tomorrow I was due to deliver a lecture on modern man and classical physics to a group of undergraduates.

All of a sudden, my world turned cold. All of a sudden, desperation was creeping up on me like a three-dimensional shadow, wrapping itself around my whole being, a doubtfulness about everything which might lead to God knows what. Even the sun was now slipping behind a huge stream of cloud and a stiff breeze filled the air. It seemed as though the atmosphere was turning in sympathy with my restlessness.

My mind was distracted by a young couple flirting along the towpath, two adolescents caught in a melange of callow sentimentality. As they passed by me they looked inquisitively in my direction and a mumble of words passed between them, followed by childish giggles. But their cheerfulness was as ephemeral as the life span of the butterfly. Here was I, a 52-year-old intellectual and they, 14-year-olds perhaps, separated by age and space, the three of us caught up in an existence that to them was here and now but to me was probabilities and predictabilities.

I could hear the village clock strike four and I coincidentally checked my watch. Mine showed three fifty-seven. Probably both were wrong, I said to myself. In fact the possibility of either of them being right was as improbable as my winning the national lottery - probably even more so. There I was again, some circuit in my brain controlling the command centre entitled 'Time Frames', an automatic start-up switch triggered by the village clock and my wristwatch.

It was time to go home. Somehow or other I had to break out of this melancholy, to rid myself of this feeling of helplessness and do some notes for my work tomorrow.

Maybe it was a reaction to all those thoughts which engulfed me down by the river but I found myself, as I paced along the towpath, considering my domestic life. It could be said that man has two lives: his working life and his home life. Some might argue that there is a third, more important than any: his spiritual life. Spirituality was a pipe-dream, an illusion, a spectre conjured up in the minds of ancient dreamers masquerading as religious men. I think it was Havelock Ellis who said: 'The whole religious complexion of the modern world is due to the absence from Jerusalem of a lunatic asylum'. That spurred me on my way as I approached the outskirts of the village.

Millie was busy cutting slices of lettuce on a chopping board when I entered the kitchen.

'Something smells nice,' I said.

'Guess' she replied.

I breathed in the spicy, aromatic smell. 'Curry of some sort,' I conjectured.

'Uh-huh. It's kofta bhoona, little meatballs in a spicy paste.'

'Excellent!'

'Nice walk, then?'

'Yeah, it was all right,' I said, dipping my finger into the curry, then tasting it. 'Beautiful. Kids about?'

'Mum still has them. She's got them till seven. You know, sometimes I don't know what I'd do without her, Mark.'

'She's a good old soul, Millie. I just wish my mum and dad were alive - they would've loved the kids.'

'As they say, darling, that's life.'

'Hmmm.' I stepped over to the wine rack. 'Aperitif?'

'I'd love one.'

I poured two glasses and handed one to my wife.

'Cheers!' she said.

'Look, I'm away into the study. Better get cracking with my notes for tomorrow.'

'Okay, I'll join you in ten minutes.'

I kissed her on the cheek and then swapped my brogues for a pair of slippers. On my writing bureau were several essays from some students which I was to return, marked up, by tomorrow. There were also one or two half-written letters and rough drafts of papers I was working on for the *New Scientist* magazine. I left that lot for later and switched on the computer. On opening my lectures folder, I selected the document which contained my lecture for tomorrow, an appraisal of classical physics in relation to present-day analytical techniques. I spent two minutes editing the draft and suddenly found myself with a mental block. Nothing would come. It was as if my brain had shut up shop for the day. The words seemed to have disappeared, evaporated into thin air like liquid oxygen. Frustrated, I shut down the computer and sat down on my favourite armchair, gently sipping my glass of red wine.

Moments later, Millie arrived. She looked gorgeous as usual, and even younger than her thirty-one years.

'Great hive of activity in here,' she offered.

'Yeah, I know.'

She sat herself down at the computer, drink in hand. 'Something wrong, darling?' she asked. 'This isn't like you.'

'I know. The fact is, everything's bothering me. Me, my job, society, the environment, people, life. Maybe I'm just tired. Tired of the routine, knowing that for the next, what, ten years, I've to stand up in front of people saying the same things at the same old times to the same old timetables.'

'But, darling, this is just not like you. What's happened? Is it me? The kids? What?'

'Darling, it's not you nor the kids,' I declared.

'Then what?' she asked earnestly.

I turned around on the chair to face her. 'If I knew the answer I'd tell you,' I replied. 'Maybe it's me that's the problem. Looking back, maybe I should have read ancient history or archaeology or something. Something that's easier on the mind.'

'Darling, physics and mathematics have been your interests as far back as I can remember. You've won prizes, awards, you're well respected in the university. That must count for something.'

'Can't you see, Millie, that's part of the problem. People might respect me for what I know, not for who I am.'

'And who are you? Or is that too deep a subject before curry?' she asked.

At least her comments brought a smile to my lips. 'When I was sitting by the river today I saw a beautiful butterfly. I'd never seen one like that before. It had these wonderful orange spots on its wings. It was a perfect example of innocence, not bothering anything, just fluttering around, being free. That's all. And then a bird appeared from nowhere and snapped it up. It was gone, eaten. Just like that.'

'So what?' she asked. 'It happens every day. There's nothing unusual about it.'

'I know there's not.'

'Well?'

'Well, I kind of empathised with that little creature, with its freedom. To all intents and purposes I'm free. I've got you and the kids, my health, a job.' I paused for a moment. 'But this freedom is false because I'm shackled to the dictates of my own actions. When I graduated, Millie, I believed passionately that physics would eventually explain everything. Here was the cornucopia of all knowledge, the tools that would eventually explain the beginning and the ending of all things. And now, twenty-three years later, I know it isn't going to happen. It's as simple as that.'

She took a sip of the wine. 'It doesn't sound simple to me,' she replied.

'No, it probably doesn't.'

I finished my glass of wine. 'Come on. Let's eat this curry.'

It was a beautiful starry evening and the moon was a half crescent. I was sitting outside on the patio nurturing a port. My son Benjamin, a boisterous eight-year-old, was with me.

'Daddy,' he said, gazing overhead, 'where do the stars come from?'

'Well, son,' I said, 'in a way they've always been here, just like us.'

'How long is that?'

'A very, very long time, son. It's so long that we call it eternity.'

'What's et... eternity, dad?' he enquired.

'It's just a word, Benjamin, to explain a long period of

time. When you're older your teachers will explain this so that you can understand it properly.'

'Why are they so bright, daddy?' he asked.

Benjamin was getting to that inquisitive age in life where everything is questioned. Questions, questions, questions. And yet I found it difficult to answer him in an English he would understand. This reinforced my conditioning, in that I could have explained these questions better using mathematics. But to an eight-year-old boy?

'It's because each and every one of these stars is like our sun. They're very hot and give off light,' I said. I knew what was coming next.

'Light, daddy? What's that?'

How does one explain electromagnetic radiation to a kid, I asked myself? Even to us physicists the idea of light could be explained using well-established principles and, is as normal, defined mathematically in terms of photons and their proportions of frequency and wavelength.

'Light, son?' I eventually said. 'Well, let's put it this way. If we didn't have light we wouldn't be able to see anything. You wouldn't be able to play with your toys, mummy wouldn't be able to cook meals and you wouldn't be able to go to school.'

He laughed. 'Oh, goody. I'd like that, daddy.'

'Well, it won't happen. As I've said before, Benjamin, you stick in at school and learn everything you can. Okay?'

'Okay,' he replied. Moments later he saw a moth fluttering around the lamp above the back door.

'Daddy, daddy!' he yelled excitedly, a moff, a moff! Look, daddy!'

Moments later it crashed into the lamp, captivated by the light, entranced by its brilliance. Benjamin was jumping up and down in a childish and vain attempt to catch it.

'You'll never catch it, son,' I said.

'Daddy, can I get it, keep it, can I? It can be my pet,' he declared.

'No, son. Moths are not like cats and dogs. And anyway they don't live long.'

'Why, daddy?'

'Because they just don't.'

Millie popped her head around the doorway. 'Right, Benjamin, time for bed.'

'No, no, I want to see the moff,' he said stubbornly.

'Never mind the moth. Now, time for bed. Come on, she said.

'Oh, all right.'

I kissed Benjamin good-night and finished my drink. It was getting rather cool now and I finally made my way to the warmth and comfort of my study. Inspiration. That was the key word. A new approach to my work, a new outlook on matter and phenomena. That was what mattered. In order to deliver the subject on a totally new level I needed a refinement of delivery and techniques.

It was when I was browsing through my bookshelves, searching for inspiration, that I came across a small volume by the Chinese thinker Chung Tsu. I took it from the shelf and sat down, opened it up and flicked through the pages. Interesting, I said to myself, very interesting indeed.

The lecture hall was packed, and there was a monotonous babble about the place. I walked into the room, approached the lectern and switched on the microphone. The voices of about 200 people petered out into complete silence.

'Good morning,' I began. 'This morning's lecture was to be about modern man and classical physics. I was going to talk about the development of the physical world, stretching from Newton's Law of Universal Gravitation to Hawking's deliberations on black holes - all wonderful stuff, I might add. I was even going to throw in a bit about string theory. But you know what? I'm not going to talk about that at all. I'm going to quote from an ancient Chinese philosopher called Chung Tsu, a man who lived around 350 BC. Chung Tsu dedicated his whole life to solving the problems of a world dominated by chaos, absurdity and change. Our physics tries to answer the same questions but to no avail, because no sooner have we solved one particular problem about the universe than another pops up in its place. Man-made theories precipitate man-made solutions. Therefore, I am going to leave you with the words of Chung Tsu: 'The fish trap exists because of the fish; once you've got the fish, you can forget the trap. The rabbit snare exists because of the rabbit; once you've got the rabbit, you can forget the snare. Words exist because of meaning; once you've gotten the meaning, you can forget the words. Where can I find a man who has forgotten words so I can have a word with him?''

I stood there gauging the reaction, which was a cross between mild shock and sudden disbelief. The audience was stunned into speechlessness, which was exactly the reaction I had intended.

'Ladies and gentlemen,' I said, coming to an end, 'the next time you are out walking in the park with your friends and you come across a butterfly, don't question the nature of it, but rather see it for what it is. Thank you.'

I quietly walked out of the university, wearing the largest of smiles, and made my way back down to the river.

A Deal Worth Closing

With a name like Cadbury, she must be sweet, he thought. Perhaps a soft centre with a milky lining, or maybe a hard nut without any pretensions, but possibly a Turkish delight with all the mystique of the East, or then a marzipan slab, dense and obtuse. Her handwriting flowed, though, where the 'i's were circled and the 't's' crossed. Just how much could be gleaned from the irrational splurge of someone's longhand? Maybe it was the way she ended her letter: 'Don't hesitate to ring me'.

Bernie Shields glanced at the telephone and licked his lips. Even the thought of it made him come out in a cold sweat. As a 'Home Improvement Executive' he oozed self-confidence when dealing with the public, but making a telephone call to a woman he'd never met or even seen definitely made his hair stand on end - well, what was left of it.

'Now, how do I start?' he said out aloud. He quickly finished the pizza he had made for tea. 'Hi, it's Bernie, here. How are you?' No, that sounded too corny. 'Pam, it's Bernie, just answering your letter.' No, that didn't sound right. 'Hi, Pam, it's your knight in shining armour here.' Never. Utterly dreadful.

He lifted the letter from the table and inspected the phone number again, as he had done for the tenth time that day. Seven seven four four four. She lived in the next town, so there was no dialling code. 'Come on, Bernie, you can do it,' he said to himself. The pile of letters he had answered lay on the table like a set of last reminders from the Electricity Board. In fact he could have written a book about all those rejections, about the fairy stories females dream up in telling you they're just not interested. Rejection and dejection were the mantles he had worn for over a year now. A broken heart was the cap he sported daily and it was due to that bitch Penny. She had even talked him into wearing a stupid carnation when they had met in the foyer of a one-star hotel. Her pugnacious laughter was hard to bear, but what really hurt was when she had stated sarcastically, within moments of their meeting, how much he resembled Billy Bunter. So, he was short-sighted, dimple-cheeked, his paunch tumbled over his belt and it wasn't his fault that he wore a forlorn smile. Christ, it was the one he was born with!

'Seven seven four four four.' He took a Kleenex from the box and wiped his brow. The telephone loomed in his sight like some mechanical ogre from another dimension. He had to do it. He could not give up now. Another Kleenex was used to wipe the palms of his hands. Damn it!

He dialled the number and momentarily hoped that the line would be engaged or she would be out. What if her mother answered the phone?

'Hello, seven seven four four four?'

Her voice sounded so mellow. Could this be the voice of a girl who had rejection in the back of her mind? Was this the beginning of the end, as usual?

'Hello? Seven seven four four four?' she said again.

'Eh... Penny? I mean, Pam?'

'Penny? No, I'm Pam. Pam Cadbury. Is this Robert?'

'Who? Robert?'

'Look, who is this? Johnnie? Johnnie, if that's you playing games...'

'It's Bernie,' he stated. 'Bernie Shields. You know, we've corresponded a couple of times.'

'Oh, Bernie. I'm sorry, Bernie, it's just that... you know, people phoning out of the blue and that.'

'You... you said I could call you. Remember?'

'Yes, I do remember. It's nice of you to call, but I didn't think it would be so soon. You caught me unawares. In fact I'm still in my nightie!'

'Oh, I didn't want to intrude or anything, Pam. I wouldn't want to embarrass you. It's just that...' He wiped his brow again.

'You sound really nervous, Bernie. You needn't be though. In fact I feel a bit nervous meself and that. Silly in't it?'

'What?'

She looked heavenwards. And then louder, 'I said it's silly, in't it?'

'No, not at all. I mean... I mean we're like strangers, aren't we?'

'You have a nice voice, Bernie. But then I suppose all the girls tell you that.'

'No no no, they don't. In fact you're the first girl...'

'Such a gentle voice, Bernie. You sound almost like double-oh-seven.'

'Double what?'

'You know, Roger Moore.'

'Oh, do I?'

'Yes you do. So what's on the agenda?'

'Well, I just thought I'd phone. You know, make contact,' he said.

'You want to meet me?' Her voice had a surprising ring to it.

'Y... yes. I would like that, Pam.'

'When?' she replied abruptly.

'Uh... uh... well, I don't really know. Do you *want* to meet me?'

'You sound so surprised, Bernie. I didn't put the ad in the paper for nuthin' you know!'

'No, of course not.'

'Let's see.' The line went silent for a moment. He could hear her talking in the background. Something about a diary.

'Tomorrow night?' she asked.

'So you're not working tomorrow night, then?'

'If I was, I wouldn't be saying tomorrow, would I, Bernie?'

He laughed. 'No, of course not. Silly billy. Where?'

'Well let's put it this way. What kind of grub d'ya like?'

Hell, I could eat anything, he thought. 'Ladies first. Why don't you make the choice?'

'Okay. Er... Italian? Chinese? Indian? Greek? Fish and chips? A burger? Do you like pizzas?'

'Yeah, yeah, I like pizzas.'

'Mind you, I prefer Chinese. But maybe you'd like to go to a hotel?'

'Okay. A hotel. The Roundtree? You know, that new one out by the golf course?'

'Okay. That sounds great by me. Eight o'clock?'

'Eight it is,' he replied.

'Right.' There followed another moment's silence. 'What'll ya be wearing, Bernie?'

'Eh, now let me see. Ah, yes, a cream three-piece suit. I'll be in the bar and I won't be wearing a pink carnation.' He tittered nervously.

Pam laughed loudly down the phone. 'You are a funny bunny, Bernie. Right. I'll be in a black coat with a white handbag.'

'Fine. Right. Well, okay, uh, right then. See you at eight.'

'Brilliant. See you then. Bye.'

'Bye.'

Wonderful. Terrific. She sounded so eloquent over the phone, so confident in her pronunciation. This could be the start of something great, he thought.

Just as he was beginning to visualise what she looked like, the phone went. He lifted the receiver and sang out, 'Hello, Bernard Shields.'

'Bernie, it's Tom. You've got an appointment at nine-thirty tomorrow morning. It looks like a goer.'

'And the address?'

'It's fifteen Ashburton Terrace, a Mrs Manley. I repeat, a Mrs Manley.'

'Okay, Tom. I'll call by the office when I've finished. Bye.'

It was a sunny morning and he went to work on a plate of eggs, bacon, black pudding, pork sausages and toast. He even washed his greying, curly hair; the first time it had seen shampoo for a week. There was a spring in his step as he got into his 1979 Ford Cortina.

Once in the car, he opened his briefcase and took out Pam's letter. He read it out aloud. One of the neighbours passed by and stared quaintly at him. 'Silly old fart,' he said, before starting the engine.

Ashburton Terrace was a cul-de-sac; one of those elaborate settings, all neatly-trimmed hedges, finely-mown lawns and disposable incomes. He stopped the car just outside number fifteen, a large semi-detached bungalow with an adjoining garage, and climbed out. He pressed the bell and waited. Through the opaque glass door he could see a woman approaching.

'Mrs Manley?' he stated proudly as the door opened. 'Window World at your service.' He handed over his business card.

Mrs Manley, fifty-something, was a large woman with

huge breasts that seemed to sag under their own weight. Her face seemed to hang as well, the jowls and double chin drooping, giving an overall Buddha-like countenance. All that beef was wrapped in a lacy black nightdress.

'Do come in,' she replied in a rather soft tone, 'I've been expecting you.'

'Thank you, Mrs Manley.'

She led him into a spacious, fitted kitchen. 'Tea, Mr Shields? I always have tea at this time of the day.'

'Well, yes, Mrs Manley. Thank you.'

'A cake? I made some beautiful currant buns yesterday. Or maybe a biscuit?'

'No thanks, Mrs Manley. I've not long had breakfast.'

Mrs Manley poured the tea. 'Milk, sugar?'

'Milk and sugar please,' he replied, and opened his briefcase.

'Now,' she said, 'there you are. A nice cup of tea.'

He was conscious of her looking him up and down and tried to put it out of his mind. 'Thank you very much. Now. Windows. Here's some of the window systems that we've found most popular recently. As you can see most of the fittings are aluminium, although those teak and mahogany ones are cheaper. Now, how many windows are we talking about, Mrs Manley?'

'Oh, it'll be the whole house, upstairs and down. Although those mahogany ones would look just divine in the master bedroom,' she said softly. 'Know what I mean?'

Bernie was taking notes now, but somehow he couldn't take his eyes off those huge tits that seemed to ogle him through the nightdress. It was the way they seemed to rest on the kitchen table like two ripe water-melons.

'I assume you'll need to inspect the rooms, Mr Shields?' she asked.

'Well I need to measure them up, Mrs Manley.'

'Of course.' She sniggered. 'You'll no doubt be very experienced in measuring things up, I bet.'

Bernie's pencil lead broke. 'Damn,' he said. 'Sorry, Mrs Manley, I didn't mean to...'

'Maybe we could start with the master bedroom,' she said, getting to her feet. 'Just leave your cup there, Mr Shields.'

'Yes... uh-huh. Okay. I'll just leave it here.'

Mrs Manley led Bernie out of the kitchen and up the stairs. She certainly had one hell of a backside on her, he thought, as he paced the stairs behind her, the big, round cheeks wobbling from side to side inches in front of his nose. And it didn't look as though she was wearing any knickers either. That cold sweat returned to his brow and, worse still, he was sure his thing was getting just a little hard. He slackened off his tie.

The spacious bedroom was decorated in many shades of pink, with a great four-poster bed draped in silk sheets. A welcome breeze wafted in through the window.

'Well, Mr Shields, what do you think?' she asked. 'Cute, isn't it?'

'Yes yes, Mrs Manley, very pretty. Uh-huh.'

'It's such a warm day, as well. Now, would you like to start measuring, Mr Shields?'

Just as he was about to reply, she lifted a pair of black silk stockings from a chair and ran them through her hands.

'Measure? Yes. Right. Now, my measuring tape, yes. Well, eh, it's downstairs in my briefcase. I'll go and get it.'

Before she could reply, Bernie was already out of the room. Mrs Manley smiled to herself and undid the lacy ties around the neck of her nightdress. Then it was a dash of perfume behind the ears. When Bernie returned she was sitting on the edge of the bed, doing her fingernails.

'Ah, Mr Shields, you're back.'

'Right, Mrs Manley, I'll get started.'

Because of where she sat, Bernie had to brush past her to get to the window, and couldn't help but notice the massive cleavage again. It looked almost threatening, as if it would gobble you up if you got too close to it.

He was just about to start measuring the width of the window when Mrs Manley lay down on the bed, on her back, and started humming *I'm in the Mood for Love*. Bernie stoically ignored her and carried on measuring. Then he dropped the measuring tape and, looking around, saw to his utter astonishment that with eyes closed, she was caressing her mammoth tits. Bernie was mesmerised, gobsmacked, his mouth agape.

'Mrs Manley, I do declare,' he eventually uttered feverishly.

'Oh, Mr Shields, it's just because it's so hot in here. Hmmmm.'

'I know but... really.'

'Come, come, Mr Shields, haven't you seen a woman

fondling her breasts before? But perhaps not breasts as big as mine?'

Bernie was still trying to carry on with his work, but he had realised that he didn't have his notepad and pencil at the ready. Maybe he should go, he thought to himself.

'Look, Mrs Manley, I've left my notepad downstairs. I'll just go and fetch it. Or maybe I should start in the kitchen.'

Mrs Manley was now simultaneously squeezing her breasts and feeling down around her navel. She tittered as Bernie, without looking in her direction, left the room.

Down in the kitchen, he quickly sharpened his pencil and pondered. There had been times before when women had hinted at sexual favours before, but this usually took place when he was about to close the deal. And right now he needed to clinch this one, as the commission would come in handy. He climbed back up the stairs and realised as he approached the bedroom door that the humming had stopped. Bernie took a deep breath and boldly entered the room.

'Mrs Manley!' he exclaimed.

Mrs Manley was still on the bed, all but naked, apart from a pair of black stockings and a massive pair of black, silk knickers. There did not seem to be a break between the two huge milk vats and the rolls of beef supporting them. The knickers stretched to breaking point in trying to contain the non-existent waistline. She had even done an extemporaneous make-up job. Had it not been for any sign of a penis, Bernie would have said this was a drag queen. She would definitely have fitted the title 'Gargantuan

Gutbucket' which he remembered from one of the Sunday tabloids.

'Well, Bernie, this is it. What do you think of my body? Hmmm?' She opened her legs a little and tried to move her lumbering hips in some kind of erotic movement. But they wouldn't move. Gravity had them firmly pinned to the bed.

'Mrs Manley,' Bernie replied, 'I really do think I should be going.' He lifted his tape measure with a trembling hand. 'There are other double-glazing companies out there.'

Bernie literally ran out of the room, charged out of the front door and sped off in his car.

The herbal bath produced the desired effect in soothing his nerves, the hair had been blow-dried and the after-shave was applied heavily. He appraised himself in the mirror and straightened his Paisley-patterned tie. It was the first time in five years he had worn the cream suit. The last time had been on the occasion of his grandmother's funeral. The upturned bottoms were decades out of date, but he was blissfully unaware of it.

The lounge bar was cosy and welcoming, all wood-panelled, with Victorian decor. The piped music was just audible. A young girl with a smiling face manned the bar counter.

'Yes sir?'

'Hi, good evening,' he replied. 'Uh, a half of bitter, please.'

Bernie popped several peanuts into his mouth and began crunching. If Pam looked half as nice as this one behind the bar, then he was in business, he thought.

'There you are. That's two pounds, sir

He gave her a two-pound coin and supped on the drink. There followed a recce of the place. Which table would they sit at? The music was nice. The wallpaper could have been a bit more upmarket. Not that busy, though. He glanced at the girl again. Yes, not bad looking at all. Nice legs, too.

Just as he was thinking of ordering another drink, he heard a clock chime eight out in the hotel foyer and, exactly on the last chime, Pam entered the bar.

Bernie spotted her immediately, at least the black knee-length coat with an imitation fur collar and the white patent handbag. He gulped. It was maybe the brunette hairdo, which was not in any particular style, or the thick horn-rimmed glasses that seemed to cover her whole face. She smiled at Bernie and tentatively stepped in his direction. She must have been all of five feet in her heels. The face was drawn, almost grey in colour and the string beads around her neck one hundred percent plastic.

She extended a hand, smiling through buck teeth. 'Bernie? I'm Pam.'

A bemused Bernie cleared his throat. 'Good evening, Pam. How are you?'

'Fine, I guess. Quite fine.' There was a glumness about her smile that indicated that she too was less than enthralled with her date's looks.

He gestured to the bar stool. 'Drink, then?'

'Yes... er, yes, I'll have a...'

'Gin and tonic? Vodka and lemonade? Rum and blackcurrant?'

'Oh, I don't think I should. Spirits make me... you know...'

'They give you a sore head, Pam?'

She hesitated. 'Uh... yes. Yes, they give me a sore head, Bernie.'

'A glass of red wine, then.'

'Well, yes. Yes a glass of red wine would be nice. Thanks.'

Bernie turned to the barmaid. 'Yes, miss, a glass of red wine for the lady.'

They smiled awkwardly at each other, which led into a drawn-out silence. There was a fleeting eyeing up of each other which only exacerbated the mutual awkwardness. Bernie cleared his throat before paying for the wine.

'So you managed the bus, then?'

'Yes. It was the thirty-nine bus. Uh-huh.'

'Oh, the thirty-nine. I see.'

'It's fine and handy.'

'Yes, well it would be, wouldn't it.'

Another half-minute of dithering silence before Pam spoke again. 'It's been another fine day today, hasn't it?' she commented.

'Beautiful. Yes, I love this weather. It's good for business.'

'Oh, of course, you're a... a...'

'Home Improvement Executive. You know the kind of thing: interior design, space management, consultancy work on art decor. We've even been moving into landscape gardening recently.'

'It sounds so interesting, Bernie, and you being an executive and all that,' she replied enthusiastically.

'Well, Pam, it's a career. Of course one doesn't get to my station in life without a track record.'

'But of course not, Bernie. Absolutely.'

He caught sight of the menu at the end of the bar and offered it to Pam. 'Well, I don't know about you, Pam, but I'm famished.'

'Me too,' she replied. After browsing through the menu she said, 'But these prices, Bernie.'

'No problem, Pam. You just choose what you want. You're dining with an executive this evening.'

She sniggered to herself. 'Of course. I keep forgetting.'

They finished their drinks and a waiter enquired if they were ready to eat. He led them into the restaurant and sat them down at a table for two. The room was all but empty and, like the lounge bar, was cosy and homely. Somehow they managed to get through most of a bottle of claret before their main dishes arrived.

'So I was the fifteenth reply you got to the ad?' Bernie enquired.

'Yes. Some of 'em were downright rude. I wouldn't even care to go into details.'

'I take it you got more than fifteen, then.'

'Yes.'

Bernie poured more wine into their glasses. 'And the final count was?'

'Thirty-nine.'

'Thirty-nine?' he said, almost worriedly.

'Sorry, Bernie, forty. Another one arrived in the afternoon post.'

'I see.'

For the first time that evening, Bernie felt dejected. Here was he thinking that maybe he had been the only one to reply to her ad. How many had she been out with up until this point? Would she entertain meeting with numbers sixteen through forty?

He was pondering this and other outcomes when the waiter arrived with their steaks. Bernie finished his glass and realised that the bottle was about empty.

'Another bottle, waiter,' he ordered.

'Bernie? Do you think we should?' she said, peppering her Brussels sprouts.

'The night is young, Pam, and gay without frivolity,' he said.

She tilted her head to the side, staring unobtrusively into his eyes, and smiled. Those buck teeth stuck out like fangs on a vampire.

'So lovely, Bernie,' she said with a sigh. 'Such sentimental words.'

She immediately took a large mouthful and got stuck into the steak. For a skinny rake of a woman, she certainly knew how to wolf down food. If only she didn't eat with her mouth open, masticating like a ravenous bull. There was nothing for it. There was no way he could ever get round to fancying this girl. And she had said in her ad that she was 'slim, graceful and attractive'.

By the time Pam had stabbed the last Brussels sprout and flung it into that wide precipice of a mouth of hers, Bernie had already ordered another bottle. Those wide, blue eyes of hers showed a tiredness about the eyelids and there was a slur developing in her speech.

The waiter arrived to clear the table and requested their dessert order.

'I'll have the peach melba, please,' Bernie said. 'Pam?'

She giggled. 'I'll have the walnut banana. And make it a big one!'

'Pam, honestly.'

'Oh, Bernie, I am enjoying this,' she replied. Then she topped up the glasses. 'I haven't enjoyed myself like this in years. Pity mum couldn't be here.'

'Your mum?'

'Yes. My mum.'

'What's she got to do with it?'

'Oh, I was just thinking about her. Do you want to hear a funny story, Bernie?'

No he didn't. In fact all he wanted was to get the peach melba and walnut banana out of the way and go home. He didn't have long to wait, because just then the desserts arrived.

'Oh, lovely,' she said. 'You know something Bernie, you men can be awful sometimes.'

'Is that right?' Bernie asked.

'Uh-huh. Take that double-glazing salesman who came around today. A real smoothie he was. You'll understand, Bernie, being in that kind of business. Well, he wasn't in the house ten minutes when he tried to... you know... oh, it's so embarrassing.' She took another slurp of wine. 'He tried to fondle her. Tried to grab hold of her ...you know.'

'Her hips?' Bernie replied jokingly.

'No no no.' She gestured to her flat chest.

'Oh, her tits?'

'Bernie!'

'Sorry, Pam, I didn't mean to...'

'Dirty sod that he was.'

'Life's full of them, Pam.'

Pam wiped her mouth after scraping around the edge of the bowl. 'That was delicious, Bernie.'

'Well, Pam, I've really enjoyed this evening. Now I'll settle up and we can be on our way.'

But he could not. He'd had too much to drink, and he was going to have to leave the car. It would have to be a taxi.

By the time they left the hotel it was dark. They had only walked about a hundred yards towards the centre of town when Bernie flagged down a taxi. He got into the front seat and Pam staggered into the back.

'Where to, mate?' the taxi driver asked.

Bernie turned to Pam. 'It's twenty-six Blenheim Street, isn't it?'

'No, not tonight, Bernie. My pal Anne is having a party there tonight. I phoned mother earlier, so I'm staying there tonight.' She leaned forward to the driver. 'It's fifteen Ashburton Terrace.'

'What?' Bernie replied incredulously. 'But that's Mrs Manley's.'

'That's right.' The driver pulled the car away. It took a moment to sink in. 'Hang on a minute. How do you know that?'

'Know what?'

'My auntie's name?'

'*Your* auntie?' he asked, totally perplexed.

'Yes. My auntie, although I call her mother because she brought me up after my real mum's death when I was a year old.' She leant over closer to Bernie. 'Is there something wrong, like?'

'No, well, yes there is, Pam. All of a sudden I've got a splitting headache. Maybe the taxi driver can drop me off first.'

Signals

'I just can't wait until later, can you?' he asked.

'No, Alain, it'll be magic,' his wife replied.

He took another mouthful of lemon meringue pie. 'Sometimes 'us' is the only thing that keeps me from going off my rocker. And this afternoon I've got three new clients to see and get the so-called case for the defence sorted out for tomorrow. Why the Establishment forces us to wear those silly bloody wigs is beyond me.'

'You can wear one of my wigs tonight if you want. That deep purple one really suits you,' she said with a wink of the eye.

'Okay, my lovely, enough of that if you don't mind. Anyway, have you decided what you're wearing tonight?'

'Ah, now, let me see,' she replied, finishing her coffee. 'Oh yes, something I bought yesterday. Of course I never told you about it. It's meant to be a surprise.'

'I'm sure it will be,' he said. 'That's what I love about you, Miriam. Always willing to please. You're so bloody good to me.'

'But then you take some pleasing, my Trojan horse, don't you?'

'And who better to mete it out?'

'I suppose I'd better get back to the hospital, Alain.'

'I'd better be going too.' He checked the bill. 'Right,' he continued, extracting the wallet from his pin-striped jacket, 'that's eighteen pounds and forty-three p.'

After paying for their midday snack, they left the restaurant and kissed each other goodbye.

It took Alain Goodman three hectic minutes to walk back to his solicitor's office in the City. He possessed a rugged handsomeness with large, watery eyes and a keen jaw and sported a permanent stubble. The thirty-three-year-old was not in the happiest of moods due to a backlog of the cases which always recurred so soon after the New Year. Mostly they were divorce proceedings, assault and battery cases and a mixture of domestic and business problems. But it was the divorce cases which seemed to pile up on his desk after the festive season. Why did so many couples find themselves splitting up during this particular time of the year? When he meditated on his own marriage he always came up with the same answer: sex. That was what it was and always would be: sex, or at least variants thereof.

He had only been back in the office two minutes when his secretary, Anne, appeared, an officious fifty-something type complete with huge bifocal spectacles and greasy hair.

'Nice lunch?' she asked, placing down on his desk a pile of papers and other correspondence.

'The usual. A light snack. Got to watch the old waistline,' he said, rubbing his tummy.

'Oh, shut up!' she replied facetiously. 'I wish I had a figure like yours.'

'Plenty of exercise, Anne. That's the secret. Rugby and jogging. Oh, and a steady diet,' he added.

'Yes, and don't I know it.'

'Anyway, did you get that letter finished?'

'It's here,' she replied, 'on top of the pile.'

'Good.'

'Anything else?'

'Yes. Now let me see.' He rummaged around on his desk and handed her several sheets of hand-written paper. 'That's a memo to Mr Higgins' solicitors. Oh, by the way, we could be doing with some more stationery.'

'Right you are, Alain. Your usual cuppa at three?' she asked.

'That'd be splendid.'

The rest of the afternoon passed normally. That was the problem, though. Everything was normal, at least on the surface. Alain's normality meant dealing with other people's problems day in and day out. Every now and then he would sit back in his office chair and snigger at the never-ending string of idiosyncrasies of Joe Public. Standing up in a court of law verged sometimes on the insane. The lengths people would go to in exonerating themselves from even the most trivial of crimes provided Alain Goodman with an endless sense of wonderment - and a very handsome income. Thank God for Miriam.

They dined on spaghetti, washed down with a delicate Bordeaux. They watched Coronation Street on the box and shared a small box of chocolates. It was getting on for nine o'clock. Miriam stretched herself on the sofa and combed her hands through her jet black shoulder-length locks. Her husband couldn't help noticing the way her nipples projected slightly inside her silk blouse.

'So,' Alain began, 'where is it?'

'Where's what?' she replied.

'You know, the surprise you talked about at lunchtime.'

She glanced at him with that seductive, rapier eye. 'Oh that,' she replied. 'Well now. It depends, doesn't it?' She drew her tongue slowly over her lips. 'Does that mean we go through next door?'

His tone of voice became more urgent. 'Yes, Miriam, it does.'

'In that case I'd better get dressed.'

She stood up and ran her hand over his crotch. 'You won't be disappointed, my Trojan horse. Now you wait there. I'll be ten minutes.'

Miriam stepped slowly out of the room and left her husband, who spontaneously began rubbing the hardness underneath his trousers. The thrill of it prompted him to go over to the cocktail cabinet and pour a glass of brandy. He returned to the sofa and waited. She had already been gone fifteen minutes when he finished the drink. What was taking so long? This was unusual. She never usually took as long as...

The door to the lounge opened suddenly. Miriam stood there, her normally attractive face transformed into a visage of evil beauty. The eyeliner was pencilled in heavier than usual, and the glossy, blood-red lipstick enhanced an already lustful pout. The blusher had been applied more deeply this time on protruding cheekbones. Gone was the jet black hair and in its place a wild, blonde Afro hairdo. Around her neck hung a studded choker. Below that was a tiny black latex bra with little holes through which her hard nipples protruded. Her ample breasts were squeezed together, deepening her cleavage. The bra was complemented by a black latex G-string, so small that her mass of pubic hair was parted in perfect symmetry straight up the middle. Her legs were finished in fishnet tights and high-heeled, knee-length latex boots. In one hand was the whip of black leather, neatly rolled up in a coil.

'Well, my Trojan horse, are you ready for it?' She walked over to him and pushed out her fanny, standing above him, domineering him.

He stretched out his hand and felt her solid thighs. She pulled away from him and then lifted one leg and dug her heel into his crotch. He groaned a little but said nothing. Next she straddled him and began rubbing her pubic mass around his nose. There was just a hint of scent.

'There now,' she said, in an accent that was deeper, as if aping a man's voice, 'how do you like it?'

He tried licking her, but she pulled away.

'Uh-uh. No, no. None of that.'

She crawled off the sofa and began rubbing the handle

of the whip under her pussy. 'Ah, that feels so good. Mmmmm!'

'Miriam, please...'

'No talking!' she commanded. And then, 'Get up!'

That was the signal. He got to his feet and began undressing. Just as he'd taken off his socks, she led him next door. The two spotlights on opposite walls of the room were pointed towards the centre. They were red in colour and gave the spartan room a glow of hazy ruddiness. The window curtains were already drawn closed as she stepped over to the corner, lifted the chair and placed it in the middle.

'Sit!' she demanded.

He did what he was told, unthinking, unmoving, but secretly loving every single second. Miriam left the room for a minute and then, from the speakers perched in two corners of the room, came the haunting melody of a Gregorian chant. The voices sounded as though they came from hell and not as a solemn applause to Christianity. She entered the room with rope and chains and began tying his hands behind his back with a length of rope. Then she stuffed a handkerchief into his mouth and tied a narrow piece of black velvet around his head, covering his eyes. Next was the chain, about ten feet in length, with links an inch long. This she began wrapping around his neck and upper body. She ended by binding his legs to the chair legs, secured by a padlock. The cold, stainless steel chain dug into his muscular frame to a level of tightness which had come about by trial and error over the past year or so.

One last thing. She began masturbating him - violently. This was the stage in the game that she had regretted for so long. How a man who possessed such a huge cock couldn't handle straightforward sex any more was an ongoing mystery to her. But she had resolved to do whatever Alain wanted, and if that meant masochism, then so be it. In fact she now got a kick out of it herself. Whilst he was tied up and happy, she would usually return to the living room and get off on a vibrator.

She dug her teeth into his hard-on and listened to his groans, spiking his balls with her finely manicured, polished nails, pulling at them, scratching them until they bled. Then it was back to his erection, which she pulled and tugged, digging her nails into the foreskin before the finale.

Her husband nodded his sweating head, which was the signal for the next part. She left the room and turned up the volume on the hi-fi system. The whip was in her right hand. As usual, his shoulders were clear of ropes and chain, and that was where she commenced. She stood about five feet away from him and began cracking the leather over his right shoulder: Crack! Crack! Crack!

He nodded again, the signal to begin on the left shoulder. The moans and groans told her that she was doing the business; tiny trickles of blood were sliding down onto his hairy chest. She flogged him relentlessly for 20 minutes, marvelling, as usual, at his fortitude in the face of such brutality.

And then another nod of the head signalled the denouement. She rolled up the whip until it was about a foot long and began violently thrashing his erect penis. The whipping by now was savage and uncompromising. The woman was howling with laughter, a tearful, crazed cackle bordering on madness. It was unremitting in intensity as she drew blood from his genitals and then he suddenly went into spasms, his whole body a torrent of pain. She stopped.

Alain lay on the bed whilst Miriam went through the procedure of nursing the many cuts on his body with cotton wool.

'Thanks,' he eventually said softly to her.

With tears running down her now cleansed cheeks, she asked, 'Happy?'

'Blissfully,' he replied.

'Good.'

As Anne entered the office the next morning, Alain quickly shoved the magazine into the top drawer of his desk. It was nine thirty.

'Good morning!' she sang.

'Good morning, Anne. And what have you got to be so happy about today?' he asked.

She took a seat. 'It's so wonderful, Alain. My daughter had a baby boy last night. Isn't it just great?'

'Well, congratulations. So you're a granny at last?'

'You know, I was just saying to Bill last night how old I feel. A granny! I never thought I'd see the day.'

'You're as old as you feel, Anne. You look just fine. Bill must be a happy man.'

'Oh, come on, Alain, flattery'll get you everywhere!'

'I don't suppose it will - will it?' He grinned. 'Anyway, what's up?'

'Right,' she said, checking her notepad, 'you've a meeting with Dobson and Dobson at eleven. Uh... Bernard wants to go over the Richmond case with you. That's at twelve thirty and there's that bigamy case this afternoon.'

'Oh, that,' he replied. 'Christ, I almost forgot all about that one.'

She tilted her head to one side. 'Cut yourself shaving this morning?'

He felt underneath his chin. 'Oh that - er, yes. I cut myself shaving. Terrible, isn't it?'

'My Bill's no worries on that score. Full beard he's got. I just love men with beards. Do you? Oops!'

'No, Anne, I don't like men with beards. In fact I don't like women with them either.'

Anne laughed a childish giggle.

'Well, I'd better get cracking,' she said, standing up.

He waited until she had closed the door and withdrew the contacts magazine from his desk drawer. The article he had written appeared on page eight: *Only When it Hurts*. Briefly, it was the attitude of one person in his quest for the limit to pain. Of course, he had used a pseudonym in explaining to the reader the fine razor's edge between ultimate masochistic sexual experience and death. In the article, of which Miriam was unaware, Alain set out the terms and conditions in reaching the final goal. It would require a noose to be placed around one's neck with the running knot being allowed to free itself in case of emergencies. He explained that he had not tried this out, but was ready for experimentation. As he browsed through the article a feeling of sexual anticipation enveloped him. He would try it out tonight.

He cleared his desk by four thirty and was back home before five. On the way home he purchased a length of one-inch diameter rope from a local ironmongery and set about tying a noose. It was harder than he had imagined. How does one set about tying a noose? But after a half-hour of experimentation he finally figured it out. Down in the garage he manufactured a bracket with a loop for the rope to go through and holes for the screws that would hold it to the ceiling. Minutes later he was in the process of inserting the last screw into the ceiling when to his surprise and horror, Miriam appeared at the door.

'And what's this?' she enquired quietly.

'Miriam! I didn't expect you home this early,' he replied. 'I had a headache.'

'You should take an aspirin or something.'

He completed the job and got down from the stool.

'You shouldn't be in here,' she said. 'It's against the rules. You're not allowed in here by yourself. You know that.'

'I know, I know. But it's this,' he said taking the pile of rope in hand. 'It's a new kind of...'

'Adventure?'

'Yes, an adventure, if you want to put it that way.'

She peered up at the ceiling. 'And that?'

'Look, Miriam, can I explain this over tea?'

She stepped over to him and flung her arms around his shoulders. 'What am I to do with you, Alain?'

He kissed her on the lips. 'Just keep on loving me. Okay?'

'Okay.' She paused, still eyeing the bracket on the ceiling. 'Pork chops and chips?'

This was a new situation. Her husband might be taking things too far. Miriam regarded the sadist thing as an extension of her love and commitment to her husband and nothing else. But then she had grown into the role and in those quieter moments away from the house, she despaired, overcome with a ponderous sense of guilt. The dividing line between pleasure and the pain she meted out to Alain was sometimes confused. When she thought about it, it felt wrong, but in the middle of actually doing it, it felt right. This might go on for years and she wasn't sure if she could sustain such an intensity of sexual exploits indefinitely.

During their meal he instructed her as to exactly what he wanted doing. They finished a half-bottle of brandy and prepared for the session. Normally, he was naked and she donned a quasi-Nazi SS uniform. However, this time she handcuffed him and arranged his penis in a leather posing pouch. The music was AC/DC, the beat raucous and driving, the guitar chords screeching. The rope was already looped through the bracket, the noose dangling maybe eighteen inches from the ceiling. She gagged and blindfolded him and helped him to mount the stool. Stepping onto a chair, she placed the noose around his neck and tightened the knot.

His head was tilted to the side to allow the rope free movement on the carotid artery.

Miriam left him as he was, went next door and turned up the music before returning. Then it was her, with the other end of the rope in both hands, tugging on the rope in time to the beat of the music. She noted his whole body straining. He was up on his toes, eyes slightly bloodshot, the veins in his neck throbbing. Pulling, now, tugging ever harder in time to the music, watching herself do it, though she couldn't help questioning herself. He lifted one knee as the signal to stop. As she let go of the rope, he fell off the stool and bent over in a heap.

'Alain? Alain? Alain!' she screamed. She took his head and cradled it in her arms, wiping his brow. 'Alain, please?'

Slowly he opened his big, brown eyes, now strained and watery. He coughed and then vomited.

'Darling, are you all right?' she asked tenderly.

'Y-y-yes,' he croaked. 'I, I... I'm fine.'

He inspected himself in the bathroom mirror. The burn marks around his neck would be concealed by his shirt collar. That was fine. The experiment had gone well. He was pleased with himself and with Miriam and the way she had handled the whole thing.

After brushing his teeth, he retired to bed and cuddled up beside his wife.

'Goodnight,' he whispered. For the first time in their twelve years of married life she did not respond.

The following three weeks were hell for Miriam Goodman.

In the past their S & M sessions had been conducted twice, sometimes three times, a week. That she could handle, and she enjoyed the dressing up and the teasing bit. She possessed a large figure, not voluptuous, but attractive. She got her strength from a once-a-week aerobics class and a spot of weightlifting. She knew she had to keep in shape, if for no other reason than to develop the muscles required for the brutality she had to inflict on her husband. But this hanging infatuation he had developed worried her. How many times had she woken up in a cold sweat in the middle of the night subconsciously thinking about it? Then lying for hours on end wondering what would happen next, what further lengths he would go to.

It was on their anniversary day that it happened. Over breakfast they exchanged cards and he presented her with a gold ring studded with opals. A table was booked at one of the city's more fashionable restaurants; the one he had taken her to the first night they met. He hinted at the location but, to his surprise, she never twigged.

During the day, Miriam seemed to dance her way around the hospital ward, tending to the patients, her attitude to everyday life brightening a little. All of a sudden the past three weeks of anxiety seemed a phantom. Alain would surely grow out of it, as naturally as a toddler grows out of its shoes.

He phoned her at three in the afternoon to see how she was doing. Fine, she said, and so looking forward to... and it slipped out: 'a normal evening'. It was the way he hung up; abrupt and cold. The table was booked for seven that night but she knew she had to get home, maybe to consume a couple of brandies to steady her nerves, because something had clicked. Call it female intuition, but she knew something was wrong. She approached the ward sister and complained of a stomach ache. Something was amiss.

His car was parked in the drive and as she entered the front door of the house, a wall of stillness confronted her. The place was so damned quiet. Without even taking off her coat, she ran upstairs and into the bedroom. Alain's work suit, shirt and tie lay on the bed. With her throat dry, and literally holding her breath, she stepped into the room. It was dark and unlit but for a column of daylight shining through the landing window.

Through the semi-darkness, Alain stood on the stool, eyes wide open, his neck slung to the side, the noose around his neck taut, the other end of the rope hitched to a makeshift bracket on one of the walls. The foam trickled on his gaping mouth. His eyes seemed to spell death itself. She was convinced he was lifeless.

Quietly and cautiously, she stepped up onto a chair and eased the rope from his neck. He seemed to grunt for a moment and intermittent spasms gripped his throat, neck and shoulder blades.

By sheer willpower, she managed to free him from the rope and place his tense body down on the floor. To her relief she caught a faint breath; it was muted and strained, but at least he was alive.

It was when she switched on the lights that the full horror came home. His entire torso was covered in tiny cuts.

Small streams of blood oozed from them and it reminded her of a passage in a book he owned, *The Knights of the Bushido* - death by a thousand cuts. It was so obvious. What was he doing to himself? Why this new crazy viciousness, this single-minded obstinacy in taking it to the limit? Didn't love come into this any more?

It took Miriam two hours to bring him round after tending the cuts and slashes that seemed to have been inflicted haphazardly. He might have undergone some ineffable erotic ecstasy, something she could not fathom even if she lived for a thousand years, but looking at him lying on the bed, covered in plasters and bandages, made her think hard about the future.

Two weeks later Alain was once more back behind his desk, having promised his wife that he would make the effort to rid himself of his sexual fantasies. She had tried to persuade him to make straightforward love, but he could not, replying that it would take time. However, behind her back, he had been keeping a record of his experiences. Unknown to Miriam, he had stolen away from work on many occasions, returning to the house through the day to do the noose trick. Unconsciously, Alain Goodman had gone from masochism to Russian roulette.

It was during a routine visit to the dentists that he read a magazine article written by an American psychologist who was a leading authority on S & M. He pointed to that nebulous region of the human mind where the sexual fantasy of the masochistic experience overlaps the death wish. It was the basis of so-called 'snuff' movies. He postulated the theory that the power and energy of the male libido could, in a sense, dominate and eventually curtail the normal sex drive, leaving in its wake an overwhelming urge for near-death experiences. This was beyond simple physical orgasm; a transformation into mental conflict with life and death. Foreplay was pain; quasi-sexual erotica death itself. It was, to use the words of the psychologist, 'the ultimate kick'.

Alain Goodman, solicitor, had made the use of words part and parcel of his profession, verbally manipulating those in the dock and members of the jury. He was well known in the legal profession for his charisma and personal magnetism and very rarely lost a case. But there was a personal battle raging in his mind, and he needed all his influence to sway Miriam in achieving the 'ultimate kick'. One last time, she had said days earlier, and then no more. This was accompanied by an ultimatum: she or his fantasies, because she wouldn't be able to handle this much longer.

Just one last time...

They dined on steaks and drank two bottles of red wine, although, as it happened, Miriam drank most of it. She imbibed the alcohol mainly as a catalyst in getting into the right frame of mind. While she was donning her latex catsuit she finished off two large brandies. For the time being she had forgotten the ultimatum and gave herself over to her role playing.

Alain was totally naked when he entered the room. 'Do it!' he ordered in a soft drawl.

'This'll be so easy,' she responded.

He placed the stool under the ceiling bracket and checked it was centralised. While he did this Miriam went next door and started a heavy metal track on the hi-fi. Entering the room, she began swaying her hips and rubbing her breasts, writhing like a demented belly dancer. He, by now, had the noose placed around his neck, ensuring that the huge knot was firmly in place, again on the carotid artery. This time there were no gags or blindfolds. This time he wanted to see things, get the visual angle, see what the 'ultimate kick' would look like.

She took up the strain on the rope and began tugging it in time to the music. The way he moaned and groaned indicated his pleasure, his neck bobbing to the side every time she tugged on it. As they had planned before the start, she now looped the rope through the bracket on the wall. Alain had pointed out that she would achieve an easier tautness on the rope without using so much energy. It was true, as she soon realised. It may have been the booze, but she was actually beginning to enjoy this, revelling in the fleeting dominance over her husband.

The music pounded relentlessly and she continuously heaved on the rope with all her might. Between the alcohol and the monotonous rumble of the music, she was becoming increasingly oblivious of what she was doing. With closed eyes, she was squawking like some tormented demon, mocking this clown on the other end of the rope, taunting, cajoling. Then a spontaneous bout of strength, a second wind, manifested itself from nowhere. Her face, neck and hair were drenched in sweat.

All of a sudden she was conscious that the music had stopped. She panted and wheezed, resting her hands on her knees. The end of the rope lay on the floor beside her. Her stomach churning and catching her breath, she looked upwards.

Fear gripped her entire body as she realised he was not on the stool. Alain Goodman lay in a heap on the floor behind the stool; he was dead.

Mr Crinshaw, defending Miriam Goodman against the charge of murder, approached the jury.

'Ladies and gentlemen, we have witnessed, during these past two weeks, an extraordinary and, if I may say so, bizarre series of events. Alain Goodman was a professional man, happily married, and a valuable member of society. His wife, Miriam, is a nurse who has on many occasions been involved in charity work and is highly regarded in the hospital where she is employed. Is Miriam Goodman a murderess? Do you think for one minute that a devoted wife like Mrs Goodman would actually contemplate murder? And murder her husband? I don't think you would.

'Ladies and gentlemen of the jury, I put it to you that this case is one not of murder, as the prosecution would have you believe, but rather one of sexual misadventure by two consenting adults. You have seen and listened to the evidence put before you. You know that Alain Goodman and his wife practised what, under normal circumstances, could be termed unnatural sexual behaviour. I put it to you that Miriam Goodman carried out the acts requested of her out of the love and devotion she had for her husband and nothing else. Ladies and gentlemen, I ask you to consider the facts of this case.

'One. Miriam Goodman carried out these, how would one put it, acts of violence on her husband because he asked her to. Two. Any physical damage inflicted on her husband was fully accepted by him. Three. Having realised what had happened that day, Mrs Goodman immediately telephoned the police and the ambulance service. Added to this she applied artificial respiration, but to no avail. Four. Finally, sexual relations between a husband and wife are of a purely personal nature. They are consenting adults, ladies and gentlemen, and the law does not and cannot stipulate what form these relations should take.

'Ladies and gentlemen of the jury, Miriam Goodman did not murder her husband. This was a fatal accident caused by one man's personal need, tragic as it might seem to you, for sexual gratification. Sexual gratification comes in many forms and contexts, some benevolent, others dangerous. Alain Goodman chose the latter. Therefore, I submit to you, that you find the accused, Miriam Goodman, innocent of the charge of murder. Thank you.'

Miriam Goodman was convicted of manslaughter and given a three-year suspended sentence. She sold the house and every piece of furniture and took up a nursing job in Dubai. She remained celibate for the rest of her life.

The Conclusion

They arrived at the door; Brad Farrar, suitcase, holdall and portfolio case in hand, and his warder with the ring of keys. A dank, grey mist skirted the prison walls as the uniformed officer opened the door.

'On the other side of this door is freedom, Farrar,' he spouted.

Farrar stopped and turned to look at the screw. 'You don't say? Well what d'you know.'

'I'll be glad to see the back of you, Farrar. It's been a long five years.'

Farrar unwrapped some gum and tossed the wrapping paper at the prison warder's shoes. 'Oh is that right now, Goosetit? Well at least I don't have to spend the rest of my life in this shit-hole - that's two divisions down from a cesspit.'

Farrar stepped through the prison door to freedom.

'You know what you are, Farrar, don't you?'

'No, Goosetit. Enlighten me.'

'A fuckin' loser of the lowest kind.'

Farrar laughed. 'I just love you when you get angry, Goosetit. Just look at you. Forty-nine years old; a trespasser against good taste.'

'Yeah, Farrar, you think you're so good with words. Your mouth'll lead you right back here and I just can't wait to see that smug, fuckin' face of yours comin' back through this door.'

'Goosetit, your feelings follow each other like the buckets on a water wheel; full one instant, empty the next.'

The warder smashed the door in Farrar's face as the latter turned towards the pavement. He checked his watch and walked further over to the roadside. 'Bastards!' he shouted. 'I'm here! I'm out! Is this supposed to be the way society welcomes a free man?'

A woman passer-by pushing a pram regarded him with disdain and quickened her step.

Further along the road he waved down a taxi. Settling down in the rear seat he told the driver, 'Ten Greenpark Way.'

Farrar tried to relax in the back of the cab, but he couldn't. The years behind bars had turned his once inscrutable smile into bothered lips, the alertness of the eye into a drowsy stare. The pigtail had been the result of a bet with a fellow inmate, but he had grown accustomed to it and kept it. And at thirty-eight, he figured he could get away with it.

The taxi dropped him off outside the small semi-detached bungalow. He paid the driver and approached the front door with diffidence. Then he searched in his pocket for the key. Habit. Of course he didn't have a front door key. There had been no need for one. The only key in his life had been the one that had locked him in that cell, three times a day for five years.

He rapped hard on the door and then looked through the letter-box. He hammered on the door knocker this time and then heard the faint sound of her voice: 'Just a minute, just a minute.'

Elsie, wearing a cotton housecoat, opened the door. 'Brad!' she exclaimed. 'Christ, I must have slept in.'

Farrar swept past her and dropped his bag in the hall. Elsie hurriedly closed the door and stopped at a wall mirror, trying to arrange her tousled, bleached perm into something appropriate to midday. She followed him into the living room. By now he was already pouring himself a large scotch.

She paused at the door. 'Brad, I'm sorry. I didn't get in until the early hours you see and I didn't...'

He was already sitting down on the settee. 'Oh you don't have to worry about me, Elsie. It's not every day you're released from prison, know what I mean?' He knocked back the scotch in one mean gulp before pouring himself another. 'Here's me, Brad Farrar, married man, criminal, dislocated wide boy from suburbia, with everything to gain and nothing to lose, and what do I come back to, eh?'

Elsie ran over to him and flung herself on his lap. 'Brad, I'm so sorry. What more can I say? I'm sorry, okay?'

'You could have been there, Elsie. It wouldn't have cost you a penny.' He drained his glass, whereupon she took hold of it.

'Here, let me,' she said, pouring him another. 'Look, Brad, you've been inside and during that time I've had to look after myself. You can't expect me to stay cooped up in here all day long, can you? And, anyway, I should be getting to work.'

He sighed. 'No, I guess I can't.'

'Right. Now what's your plans?'

'Plans? In a few days I'll start thinking about plans.' He was now exploring her soft, spongy hips, and then opening her housecoat, licking her nipples. 'It's been a long time, Elsie. God, has it been a long time.'

In an instant of doubtfulness, she eased his head away from her. 'Not now, Brad,' she said with a smile. 'Maybe you need something to eat. I've got some lamb chops in the fridge.'

Brad was by now stripping the coat from her upper body, kissing her large, round breasts and simultaneously letting his hand slip down between her legs. 'Come on, Elsie, let's do it now, on the floor. Come on.'

She gently shoved him away and pulled the coat around herself in a protective manner.

'What the fuck's up with you?' he yelled. 'Gone frigid all of a sudden? Eh?'

'Look, Brad, it's been a long time. I can't just turn it on like that. It's like... it's like we're... we're strangers.'

'Strangers? You're my wife, for God's sake. I've been

locked away for five fucking years. Do you understand that? Huh? Do you know what it's like being locked up? Do you?'

'Brad, keep your voice down, please,' she begged.

He went silent all of a sudden. 'Ah. Right, I get it,' he continued in a more concentrated voice. 'You don't need sex because you've been getting it somewhere else. Is that it?'

'No, Brad!' she pleaded.

'Five years is a long time to go without it. Of course. How could I be so stupid? I'm away, shut up in a cell, cut off, not knowing any the better. And there was me thinking Elsie wouldn't be unfaithful. No, not good old Elsie. So where were you last night?'

She squinted at him from the side of an eye. 'If you really must know, I was with Senga. We went to the Thousand Oaks Club. They had a promotion night and disco. We had a meal, a few drinks, that was all. Look, Brad, nothing happened. And, anyway, we've got more important things to discuss.'

'Like what?'

'Like Micky Grizzard wants to see you.'

'Micky Grizzard? That turd.'

'He says he wants to help you. Wants you to get back on your feet. Brad, we all want to help you. You must understand that.'

'Elsie, you seem to forget that I've spent the last five years doing exactly that. I don't need any help from a double-crossing bastard like Grizzard.'

'And you think an Open University degree's going to get you a proper job?'

Farrar stood up and poured himself another whisky. 'That was a means to an end. In fact I enjoyed doing it. You felt as though you'd achieved something. But then I'm one of the world's great achievers, ain't I?'

'So you went on painting?'

'Of course. Got to keep me hand in there, Elsie. Oh, yes. Counterfeiting was an excellent grounding all right, but I've moved on to more legal things now. Better things.'

The telephone bleeped. 'I'll get it,' Elsie said. While she tended to the phone, Farrar tended to the whisky bottle. 'It's for you,' she said. 'It's Micky Grizzard.'

He stepped over to the phone.

'Yeah? Not bad, how's yourself? And the wife? Haven't got any plans at the moment... Christ I'm just out, Micky... Look, I can't talk about things like that at the moment... When? Five o'clock? Okay, I'll be there. Right, cheerio.'

'What does he want?' Elsie asked.

'Wants to see me. Today. At five.'

'And you're going to see him?'

'Well, he's buying. Maybe I'll have some interesting things to talk to him about.' He set about pouring the whisky. 'Catching up on what's new. Know what I mean?'

Farrar eventually entered the bar at five minutes to six. Grizzard the Lizard, as he was known in the business, a slimy reptile of a man with a patch over one eye, was sitting in a corner reading an evening newspaper. He caught sight of Farrar entering the pub.

'Brad!' he shouted, 'over here.'

As Farrar walked over to the table, Micky was already on his feet. He extended his hand. Farrar shook it limply.

'It's great to see you, man. How's tricks?' said Micky.

'Well, I'm here. I thought you might say something like 'long time no see'.'

Grizzard laughed. 'Oi, Bill!' he shouted to the barman, 'two pints.' Then to Farrar, 'Come on man, sit yourself down.'

Farrar sat down opposite his old partner. 'So what's happenin'? What's the latest?'

'What do you mean? There isn't any 'latest.' That's what's latest!'

'Well, how's Elsie?'

'Fine I guess.'

'Bet she was over the moon getting you back and all!'

The barman arrived with two pints of pale ale. Grizzard gave him a ten-pound note and told him to keep the change, and then, supping the brown nectar, he paused. 'Car goin' well, Brad?'

Farrar stared him right between the eyes. 'How did the cops know about the rendezvous, Micky? Because some bastard told them. Right?'

'I told you before, Brad, they were tipped off. Jenkins was involved. It was one of his men that blew the whistle. No bullshit, Brad. It was Jenkins. That's definite.'

'I don't fuckin' believe you, Micky. Jenkins wanted to make the peace. But you screwed him out of that security job. Remember?'

Grizzard took out two cigarettes and lit them up.

Handing one to Farrar he said in a conciliatory tone, 'Okay, fair's fair. I admit that I pissed him off but he didn't have to go blowin' the whistle on me.'

'On you? Fuck, it was me who did the time, Micky. I was the one caught red-handed. Half a million quid, Micky!'

'I know, I know, I know. Listen,' he said, his voice dropping off to a semi whisper. 'We've got a contact in Zurich who's willing to do a deal with me. It's for five million US dollars in hundred-dollar bills. I want you to handle it, Brad. You're the best in the business. What d'you say, man?'

Now Farrar supped on his pint. 'I'll say one thing about you, Micky. You can be a really cheeky bastard at times. D'you think I'm crazy? I mean, really? Do you think I'm so stupid to get caught up in all that shit again?'

'Look, Brad. It's worth seventy-five grand. You just do the plates. There's no paper involved. No pissin' around with inks, presses, none of that shit. Not like the last time.'

'And if I say no?'

Grizzard leaned over the table. 'Think about it, Brad. I'll give you a couple of days. Take your time. Don't rush things. But let me know, buddy. Okay?'

Farrar took another swig at the glass and stood up.

'You don't have to leave, Brad,' Grizzard remonstrated. 'Hell, we could have a session. Just like the old times. No?'

'I'll be in touch within forty-eight hours.'

Farrar placed the glass on the table and quietly left the bar.

By the time he awoke the following morning Elsie had gone off to her job as a secretary at the town hall. He slept a dreamless night, but also a sexless one. How many times had he lain in that bunk bed, dreaming of his first night after his release, cuddling up to his wife, kissing her, feeling her, making love to her? Endless nights of sex he had dreamt of, making up for lost time. As he lay on the bed, his eyes fixed on the ceiling, he could not comprehend why she had rejected him.

He breakfasted on two hard-boiled eggs, toast and coffee before opening up his portfolio. The paintings, several water colours and the rest oil, were what he termed 'immune imaging', mental extrapolations, he would go on to explain to his fellow inmates, who, on the whole, thought he was on the verge of a nervous breakdown. But Farrar, during an open arts day organised by the prison governor and local community groups, found an acquaintance in one Matthew Sydney-Fowles, a prominent art dealer and critic. It was not long before Farrar began painting on a commission basis for Sydney-Fowles, the money being invested in a trust fund.

He retired upstairs to his studio and entered the darkroom, the door of which was hidden behind a wardrobe. Here were concealed all the tools of his former trade: aluminium plates, rollers, inks, paper and camera equipment. He turned to a drawing table and opened one of the top drawers. Inside were neat little piles of finely-packaged crisp currency notes from all the developed countries in the world.

After a half hour or so he was back on the easel, continuing a painting he had begun several weeks before his release. He had already given it a title: *The Conclusion*. This was his own interpretation of bedlam, of the upheaval and inner turmoil of cell life; the slopping out of excreta, the putrid smell of urine, the jangling of keys, the echoing of footsteps, the boredom associated with daily jogs around the yard. Then the desires; sex, booze, the innocence which lies between the pages of girlie magazines, soft porn movies, a decent meal, spending money, the simplicity of going to the newsagents in the morning for the newspaper. All of this and more was portrayed in the characterization which was *The Conclusion*.

He heard the telephone bleep downstairs. That would probably be Elsie, he thought. Or maybe Grizzard. That thought made him want to forget it. But it continued to bleep.

'Yes, hello? Matthew, hi, how are you?' he asked with a smile. 'Yesterday? Oh, all right... Well, you know how things are... Painting? Yes, I'm working on that one at the moment... Yeah, you can have another look, no problem. When? Tonight? Okay, right... Eight o'clock? Fine, see you then. Bye.'

He gently placed the receiver down, paused, and skipped back upstairs to his studio.

'What d'you mean you're going out?' Farrar asked.

Elsie was at a wall mirror in the living room putting the final touches of gloss to her lips. 'The accounts department, Brad. They've got a budget meeting and I have to be there. It's all part of the job. The council calls it loyalty. It's expected of you.'

'And when does this so-called meeting finish?'

'When it finishes.'

'In other words you don't know when you'll be back. Is that it?'

'Hopefully around eleven. But you've got that chap... what's his name?'

'Matthew Sydney-Fowles.'

'Yeah, him. Eight o'clock, is it?'

'I need a drink,' Farrar said in disgust.

Elsie took one last look in the mirror and lifted her handbag. 'Well I must be away, Brad. See you.'

Farrar continued to pour himself a drink. Without looking in her direction he mumbled something that passed for a 'goodbye'. He waited until the front door closed and returned to the studio. *The Conclusion* would perhaps require another week's work and then he could commence his next project, a rendering of life on the outside.

The thought suddenly struck him; what was he going to do about the job for Grizzard? He decided to sleep on that one and set about sorting his brushes and palette.

It was just after eight o'clock when he heard the front door. Quickly, he wiped his hands on a towel and hurried downstairs. On opening the door he was confronted by a larger-than-life fop of a man in his mid-fifties, with unruly silvery locks and a face as round as the moon; Matthew Sydney-Fowles.

Farrar smelt the air and took in an aromatic scent akin to cinnamon. Then he sniggered at the polka-dot cravat which the art dealer and critic sported, tucked inside a shocking pink silk shirt.

Sydney-Fowles stepped forward and embraced Farrar, kissing him on both cheeks in the process.

'Okay, okay, you don't have to overdo it,' Farrar said with a smile.

'Brad,' he said, 'how are you?' He looked Farrar up and down before stating, 'My, my, my, just look at you. So fit and healthy, darling, fit indeed.'

'Come on in,' Farrar said.

He led Sydney-Fowles into the living room and beckoned him to sit down on the settee.

'Drink, Matthew?'

'Let me see now. Port. Yes, I'll have a nice glass of ruby port, Brad.'

'Port?'

'Yes, lovey, a port. A proper gentleman's drink.'

'Sorry but port is out of the question, Matthew. Could I interest you in a beer, a scotch?'

'Beer? Scotch? How utterly dreadful. Oh, make it a shandy then, and go easy on the beer.'

Farrar fixed his guest an ale shandy and poured himself a whisky. 'There you are, Matthew.'

'A frightfully disgusting beverage, darling, but it'll suffice.'

'Going by your dress, I see you haven't changed much,' Farrar said.

'No, just the same old me, Brad. We're a dying breed, my man, like a nearly-extinct species.' He took a delicate sip on the glass and squirmed. 'God awful stuff. Anyway, to business. *The Conclusion*? How's it coming along?'

'It's nearly finished, as a matter of fact.'

'Great. Splendid. The last time I saw it was, oh, what, maybe half-way complete. I'm telling you, darling, that'll make the showpiece in the exhibition. The Assembly Rooms are all booked and...'

'Hey, hang on a minute, Matthew. What's this about an exhibition? Assembly Rooms?'

'Brad, darling, you needn't worry about a thing. It's all arranged. Look upon it as a coming home present. I've been working on it for five weeks and I have the finance all arranged. An exhibition of your work is booked for showing next month from the ninth to the twenty-eighth. I'm so excited, Brad! What I do need is to have your work photographed so that we can go ahead with the brochure. I'm telling you, lovey, you'll be a sensation. I just know it.'

Farrar lay back in the armchair and combed a hand through his hair. It was so sudden. 'Well, what can I say. I'm... I'm honoured, flabbergasted even.'

'Listen, Brad. That exhibition we did at the prison was only a minor success. It was more a PR exercise. The important people, the big guns, the big noises, weren't there. Now I've been putting your name about, Brad, dropping it into conversations at dinner parties. Many people in the business are ready, Brad. They want to see this talent. Your career could be limitless. You could go all the way to the top!'

Farrar lit up a cigarette and looked at this quaint man sitting across from him. It all seemed to hit him so fast, so soon after prison. But then he didn't know any better. After five years behind bars, it would take to time to readjust to everyday life. What the hell...

'Next month?'

'Next month, darling.'

'Okay. Why not.'

'Spiffing, Brad, absolutely splendiferous.' Farrar instinctively took a mouthful of shandy and squirmed again. 'Now leave everything to me. By the way, your good lady?'

Farrar rose to his feet and ignored that question. 'Would you like to see *The Conclusion*, Matthew?'

'But of course.'

Sydney-Fowles followed Farrar into the studio. 'Well, there it is,' he said.

The painting, four feet by six feet, sat on two easels in the centre of the floor. Sydney-Fowles stood motionless, riveted to the spot, casting his expert eye seemingly over every brush-stroke. Then he took two paces backwards, again moving his head to the side and then squinting, as if focusing on some minor detail.

'This, Brad, is a masterpiece. A quite extraordinary piece of work. I mean it's so outrageous in its simplicity and yet extravagant in meaning, deep in places and so shallow in others. You've captured everything here, Brad, it's a real *tour de force*. Magnificent.'

'It's as good as that?'

He turned to look at Farrar. 'I've been in this business for thirty years, darling, and I know a painting when I see one and this is... well... I'm lost for words.'

'So,' Farrar said, 'next month?'

Sydney-Fowles, still ogling the painting retorted, 'Yes, next month.'

They sat at the kitchen table drinking coffee. She was still in her dressing gown and he was already dressed and reading the morning newspaper. He got to his feet and poured another coffee.

'I'll have one too, Brad,' Elsie said, holding out her cup. He topped it up. 'You're very quiet, Brad. What's up? Uh?'

'Good meeting, was it?'

'Yeah, it was fine.'

'Must have went on a bit then?'

'Yes, it did.'

He glanced up at her from the paper. 'Until two in the morning?' he asked, this time with more venom to his voice.

'Brad, sometimes these meetings do go on. You know what local councils are like.'

'That's the point, Elsie. I do not know. What I do know is that I wanted us to have... to make love last night. Don't you remember?'

'Brad, I'm tired, and I think I should be getting ready for work.'

Elsie went over to the kitchen sink with her cup with him at her heels. He grabbed her with both arms. 'If you're seeing somebody behind my back... '

She pulled away from him and shouted, 'Brad, you'll get what you want but only when I'm ready for it. Now, I really must go.'

'And you don't want to know what Matthew said last night? No, because you're not fucking interested - are you?'

'Look, Brad, we'll discuss it later, all right?'

What was the point, he thought. But maybe she had a point. Maybe women couldn't turn it on after five years. He had to give her the benefit of the doubt. He stopped her before she went upstairs to get dressed.

'I'm sorry, Elsie, I didn't mean to raise my voice.'

'No problem, Brad. Just give me some more time. Okay?'

He kissed her gently on the lips.

'Okay. Now you'd better go.'

Matthew Sydney-Fowles phoned Farrar later that day suggesting they meet at the Assembly Rooms. He wanted to introduce him to the director of the establishment. It was about planning the exhibition and a possible auction of some of his paintings. The meeting was arranged for five. That would come after the meeting with Grizzard, whom he had phoned earlier in the morning. Yes, he would take on the job of doing the dollar plates. And, yes, the plates would be handed over within two weeks. Two important decisions in the space of forty-eight hours. But did he need the money? Because according to Sydney-Fowles, he was going to make money out of the exhibition, maybe more money than he had ever dreamed possible. He put it down to keeping his hand in, keeping all options open. He had learned that lesson often enough in prison - never close any doors behind you. As for Elsie, well, that was an enigma that would hopefully unravel by itself.

Grizzard sat in the same corner of the pub and greeted Farrar with that false pomposity that hung around him like a bad smell. Farrar brought his drink over to the table.

'Nice to see you again, mate,' Grizzard said, extending his hand in welcome.

'The answer is yes, Micky. I'll do the job for you. As I said, you'll have the plates in two weeks. Have you got the bills?'

Grizzard withdrew a buff envelope. 'There's several notes in there, Brad. They're the best my friends could come up with. But at the end of the day, a hundred dollar bill doesn't change much.'

Farrar inspected one of the notes, holding it up to the light, then feeling it with thumb and forefinger. 'Nice example, Micky. I don't see any problems here.'

'I knew you'd say that, Brad. So a couple of weeks?'

'Thereabouts. And the money?'

'Cash on delivery, mate. Twenty-five grand as agreed.'

'One thing, Micky. No surprises.'

'Look, Brad, you're talkin' to Micky Grizzard. When it's done we'll have a celebration. Bring the wife along. It'll be nice to see her again.'

'I'm sure she'll be delighted.'

'She's a nice lass, Brad. Salt of the earth.'

'If you say so. Right, well, I've got to go now. I'll be in touch nearer the time.'

Farrar stood up.

'By the way, Brad. Not a word to Elsie on this. Right?'

Farrar nodded and left the pub.

The following two weeks were frantic. *The Conclusion* was finished, the photographs for the exhibition brochure were taken and the initial work on the forged dollar bills began. This required taking four separate photographs on a process camera of the finest clarity, much sharper than the usual family snapshot. The photographs were taken through special filters to separate out the three primary colours. The negatives of these were exposed through screens on a plate maker and transferred to the special aluminium plates. Farrar experimented with this process during the two weeks and ran them through his offset litho press. By trial and error he came up with a standard of forgery that equalled the quality of the bills Grizzard had given him in the pub that day. The plates he eventually hid, and all the equipment was wiped down and taken to a rubbish dump; he left nothing to chance.

However, he and Elsie were as remote from each other as ever. What he could not understand was that when he threw tantrums, and there were quite a few during this time, she seemed to just stand there, like some bronze statue, and take it. What did not help was the fact that he worked on the forgery late at night and possibly this was one of the reasons for the tension. But how was he to tell?

It was a Saturday afternoon and he was to meet Sydney-Fowles at the Assembly Rooms for a preview of the layout of his work. The art dealer met him on the stairs leading to the hall and ushered him in. The rooms were all on one level, of which there were six.

'What do you think, darling?' Sydney-Fowles asked as they walked into Room One.

Farrar looked on in amazement. All his paintings were now framed. 'What can I say, Matthew? Just brilliant.'

They began to stroll around the room. A set of leather-backed chairs had been arranged in the centre.

'By the way, here's the brochure,' said Sydney-Fowles, handing the glossy booklet to Farrar.

'Very professional, Matthew. I like it,' Farrar enthused, thumbing through the pages.

Sydney-Fowles was about to comment on one of the paintings when in walked Zoe, a colleague of his, a thirty-year-old New Age-type woman complete with tweed skirt, duffle coat and sandals. Sydney-Fowles kissed her on both cheeks.

'Zoe, it's a delight to see you, lovey. Now this,' he stated with much ceremony, 'is Brad Farrar. Brad, Zoe.'

They shook hands.

'It sounds corny, I know, but Matt really has told me all about you. You must be excited,' she said.

'I am, I am. Of course. You're obviously in the business?'

'She's the authority on English eighteenth century painters,' Sydney-Fowles interrupted proudly. 'Isn't that right, darling?'

'Your flattery, Matt, is as runny as yoghurt. Don't listen to him, Brad.'

'Oh, I believe him, Zoe. Anything he says,' Farrar said grinning.

The three of them began wandering around the room, with Farrar giving potted histories of his work and his inspirations. They ended up in Room Six, a small room in comparison to the others, which was reserved wholly for the display of *The Conclusion*. Farrar spoke for thirty minutes explaining the background to the painting and the inherent meanings behind it.

Finally Sydney-Fowles departed, leaving Farrar and Zoe alone. Half an hour later they were sitting in a nearby wine bar with a half-empty bottle of Chablis in front of them.

'You know who you remind me of?' Brad asked, right out of the blue, with a cheeky smile on his lips.

'Go on then,' Zoe replied, looking closer at the handsome painter opposite.

'I mean, from the first moment I set eyes on you... that hair, the dreamy eyes and that symphonious look of innocence.'

'Symphonious?

'Like, you know, tuneful, like a sweet melody.'

'God, you sound more like a writer than an artist.'

'Maybe it's madness.' He took another mouthful of Chablis. 'I think it was Dali who said that there was only one difference between a madman and him. The madman thinks he is sane. He knew he was mad.'

Zoe took a sip of the wine. 'You, mad? And as for thinking I look liked who?'

'Oh, yes, Janis Joplin.'

Zoe laughed, but it was more of a snigger. Mentally, she turned back the pages of time. She was enjoying this banter. 'Janis Joplin? You crazy?'

'Well, maybe. I guess being banged up for five years alters one's sense of perception.'

'Yeah,' Zoe replied. 'A bit like Janis Joplin. Yes, the Queen of Psychedelia or something.'

Brad finished his drink, poured another and topped up Zoe's glass. 'That prison cell could have been classified as a bad trip. It would have driven Janis insane. I mean the number of nights I existed in that solitary eight-by-six plot of desperation, some weeks locked up for 23 hours, eating stinking food, drinking contaminated water. I shall spare you details of the... well, toilets.'

There was a far-off look in his eye, as if he was recalling those hellish times. Zoe instinctively took his hand in hers. 'Oh, Brad, what can I say?'

He turned his gaze to look at her. He smiled and she responded. It was one of those rare fusions of desire, a resonance of feelings; something proverbially clicked.

'Anyway that was how things panned out inside, Zoe.'

'But you had your painting. That must have helped,' she said.

'... and that was how I ended up inside, Zoe.'

'But you had your painting. That must have helped,' she said.

'I don't know what I would have done if it hadn't been for my work and the degree. I've seen grown men literally on the verge of topping themselves in that place. Believe me, Zoe, it's not the kind of place you would want to spend the rest of your life in. Some more?' he asked, taking hold of the bottle.

'No, I'd better be going.'

Farrar glanced at his watch. 'Twenty to nine. I'd better get moving too.' He got to his feet and helped her on with her coat.

'Me, too, I suppose.'

Farrar got to his feet and helped her on with her coat.

'The age of chivalry is not dead,' she said.

Their eyes met for an instant. 'I'll see you to... are you driving?'

'I'll be taking the bus actually. Why?'

'Could I see you to the bus stop?'

They were just at the door. She stopped and turned. 'You're very charming, Brad. I... I just thought I'd let you know.'

Farrar took her by the arm and led her out. It was dark now and the walk to the bus stop took ten minutes. Almost directly across from the bus-stop was an Italian restaurant. Zoe was telling Brad about her career as an art dealer and the column she wrote for a Sunday supplement when his eye caught two figures leaving the restaurant.

'...and I got paid twenty-seven thousand a year... Brad? Something wrong?'

Brad's step had frozen, his mouth agape. One of the two figures was Micky Grizzard. The other was Elsie. Grizzard was holding Elsie's hand and leading her to where his Daimler was parked. As Brad watched, he opened the door for her and kissed her on the lips. Even from a distance, he could hear his wife tittering like a schoolgirl.

'No, it's nothing, Zoe.' Brad paused for a moment, his mind working through all the ramifications of what he'd just witnessed. 'Zoe,' he continued, 'would you like to dine with me tomorrow night?'

'Yes,' she replied instantly, 'Why not?'

The exhibition opened on Monday afternoon and within

forty-eight hours Sydney-Fowles had taken orders for half of Farrar's paintings. The artist himself had been approached directly by collectors and private individuals to acquire his talent for other paintings. Between Sydney-Fowles and Farrar, they agreed that *The Conclusion* would be put on auction the following week, such was the intense interest in this particular work. Sydney-Fowles reckoned that the painting might sell for six figures. By now Farrar was getting increasingly dubious about the forgery job he had completed for Grizzard.

But there was Elsie...

Elsie and her husband sat at the breakfast table the following morning. 'So the exhibition's going along well?' she asked.

'If you had the interest to come along you wouldn't be asking that question, would you?' he replied sardonically.

'Well, I'm busy just now, what with these bloody budget meetings and that. But I promise I'll come along on Saturday morning. Okay?'

'Suit yourself. Oh, one thing though. Micky Grizzard's coming around this evening. We're having a meeting about plans and things.'

'Oh? When?'

'Well, the exhibition finishes at seven tonight, so it'll be eight o'clock or thereabouts.'

'I see,' she said thoughtfully. 'Well, I should be back by then. It'll be nice to see Micky again.'

'Yeah, we can have an old chinwag. Catch up on old times.'

'What's he coming for anyway?' she stated as an afterthought.

'As I said, plans, looking towards the future. Where we go from here, that sort of thing.'

'Ah, right.' She glanced at her watch. 'I must be going, then.'

'So it'll be eight o'clock. You'll be here?'

'Yes. Fine.'

Later that day, Sydney-Fowles, with much bravado and self-congratulation, informed Farrar that *The Conclusion* was being auctioned on Saturday evening. There was no reserve price on the painting, an illustration of Sydney-Fowles' faith that the bidding would go into five figures and probably six. Farrar's dubiety about Sydney-Fowles' assessment of the situation was tempered by the growing attention he was receiving from Zoe. This, more than anything else, was preoccupying his concentration. But still there was Elsie.

After the Assembly Rooms had closed, he accompanied Zoe to the bus-stop and got a taxi home. His attention was drawn to the living room light, which was on. Strange, he thought. Or had he left it on before leaving this morning?

Micky Grizzard sat on a chair in one corner of the room drinking what looked like a whisky, and Elsie was on the settee. Farrar noted the change of dress. She had gone to work in the morning wearing a pair of leggings. She now wore a pleated skirt.

'All sitting comfy, are we?' Farrar enquired.

'Brad, how are you?' Grizzard offered. 'Sorry, mate but I

haven't had the time to get round to your exhibition. In fact I was just sayin' to Elsie that we could come around tomorrow. Elsie?'

She sat rubbing her hands together. 'What? Yes... yes, we could do that.'

Farrar removed his jacket and threw it over the settee. Then he sat down across from Grizzard. 'Yeah, you just do that, Micky. Funnily enough Elsie's also been too busy to come along. It's all those council meetings and things.'

'Look, Brad, about the job. I told Elsie about it, you know, what with it being ready. Well,' he laughed, 'I assume it's ready?'

'Oh, it's ready all right. But you see, Micky, there's strings attached.' He got up and went over to the cocktail cabinet and poured himself a large whisky.

'What do you mean 'strings'?'

Once Farrar had returned to his chair he continued. 'Big strings, Micky. You see I have done this job for you completely free of charge.'

Grizzard let out a flustered laugh. 'You've got me there, Brad. We agreed. Twenty-five grand. Right?'

'That's correct. In a way I'm glad you told Elsie, because she's part of the deal.'

'What are you talkin' about, Brad?'

Farrar looked at Elsie. He got to his feet. 'I'll be down in a minute.'

Elsie butted in. 'Where are you going, Brad?'

Farrar left the room to go upstairs. He returned moments later carrying a plastic carrier bag. 'You can have this, Micky. It's the job. But there's a condition attached.'

'There's no conditions, Brad. We have a deal,' Grizzard stated vehemently. 'So no bullshit, right?'

'I'll come straight to the point, Micky. You can take this,' Farrar said, tossing the carrier bag on to the settee, 'and you can take my wife while you're at it.'

'What are you talking about, Brad?' Elsie asked.

'I think your husband's a bit barmy, Elsie.'

'Take her with you, Micky. Christ knows how many times you've had her anyway. She's yours.' He turned to Elsie. 'You and Micky will make a nice couple, Elsie. Council meetings my arse!' he shouted. 'You were with that bastard, weren't you?'

'Hey, Brad, now just wait a...'

Farrar turned to Grizzard. 'No, you just wait a minute. Now, I'll say it again. You've got the job and I don't want the money. What I do want is that you take my wife. That's the price for the job. And don't worry, Micky, I won't blow the whistle on you. Just take her and get the hell out of my house.'

Elsie, now in tears, got to her feet. 'Brad, I'm sorry. But five years is a long time. A woman has needs, Brad. I didn't mean to be unfaithful but... '

'Shut up!' Farrar screamed. 'Just pack your bags and go!'

'Come on, Elsie,' Grizzard said, lifting the bag and rising, 'I don't think you'll get much sense out of 'im.'

'By the way, Micky, don't try and double-cross me. There's absolutely no traces of that job in the house and the plate's clean. I'll tell you what, though, you're doing me a huge favour taking that thing away. Maybe some day you'll regret it.' At which point Elsie ran upstairs to start packing.

The three of them, Farrar, Zoe and Sydney-Fowles, enjoyed a fine Chinese meal in celebration of the success of the exhibition, but more so to celebrate the selling of *The Conclusion* . An American dealer had beaten off fierce competition in buying it for £187,000. Sydney-Fowles topped up their glasses with champagne.

'Brad, this is for your health, future success and,' he said, glancing at Zoe, 'eternal happiness, perchance?'

Zoe aimed a shy smile at Farrar and asked, 'One thing, Brad. Something I've been meaning to ask you. What's become of your wife?'

'Well, Zoe, let me put it this way. She ran away with a forgery.' Farrar gulped down the champagne and ordered another bottle.

Heads You Win

The stage was clothed in darkness and the audience hushed. The solitary spotlight picked out a head, that of a woman. Her long, golden locks shimmered under the light. The spotlight widened to embrace the figure of Karl Hesketh, dressed in tops and tails, the Van Dyke beard trimmed to perfection and complementing fully his wiry, greying, swept-back hair. The head on the guillotine animated slowly and wriggled uneasily, and then came the muffled roll of the timpani drum, starting off as a low rumble and then developing into a thunderous crescendo.

The hand latched on to the lever and pulled it down with great conviction, and the razor-sharp blade whirred down and severed the head. Blood spurted everywhere as the head rolled off the block, tumbled onto the stage and came to a stop close to the executioner's feet. Shocked gasps and screams echoed around the theatre, cries of disbelief were yelled out, even from the small orchestra in the pit. Simultaneously, the stage lights were killed. Several people occupying the front stalls passed out at the incredible illusion they had just witnessed.

Was it an illusion? Everyone knew that Karl Hesketh was the master of the magical shock, the supreme wizard of suspense, but this was taking magic to new, unexplored depths of depravity, or so it seemed.

Hesketh reappeared several moments later with the girl; she had been picked from the theatre audience earlier. As she strolled off the stage, the audience began to clap and cheer. A standing ovation ensued, whilst Hesketh stood on the edge of the stage, arms aloft, smiling and then bowing, delighting in the adulation. He quietly walked off the stage to much clapping and congratulation from stage hands and other theatre personnel.

Inside his dressing room was a bottle of champagne and a piece of paper on which was scribbled the message, 'See you at 11.00 - the usual place, Cindy'. Hesketh took the piece of paper and set it alight with a match.

There came a knock on the door. 'Just a minute.' He quickly dusted the paper ash into the metal waste-basket. 'Come in,' he ordered.

His agent, Bob Sharples, let himself in to the dressing room. He would be thirty-ish, clean-shaven and fair-haired, portly with dimpled cheeks.

'That one knocks them over every time, Karl.' He sat down on a chair and lit a cigarette. 'Come on, how's it done, eh?'

Hesketh twiddled with his beard. 'Bob, Bob, Bob, how many times do I have to tell you?' He was removing the silver paper from the champagne bottle. 'That illusion took me ten years to perfect, Bob. Every minute detail I designed myself: the blade, the head block, the mechanics of the machine. Even though I say it myself, the head block was a stroke of pure genius.'

Sharples interrupted, 'But the heads, Karl, just how the hell can you plan that? I mean they're different. Every volunteer you use, all totally different!'

The champagne cork popped. 'A drink, Bob?'

'On you go.'

Hesketh poured two drinks and handed his agent one. 'You know Bob, a couple of years ago I had the owner of the Golden Desert Hotel in Las Vegas approach me one evening at a dinner party. He took out his cheque book and asked me to name my price for owning the rights to this illusion. Silly man. That's the problem with those Yanks; think they can buy you - everything's for sale. You see, Bob, in this game everybody wants to be one step ahead of you. It's almost like civil war. And you know something else? Those self-same people would try to destroy you as soon as your back was turned.'

'That's old hat, Karl. I mean I've been in this game long enough to understand that.' He took another sip on his glass. 'Hey, nice fizzy pop!'

'But then you haven't been in this game as long as I have, Bob. I'll give you another twenty years. Anyway, now if you'll excuse me, I'll clear up here.'

Hesketh finished his drink while his agent pulled out his diary. Sharples was thumbing through the pages when Hesketh turned to his make-up bag, from which he withdrew a Smith and Wesson .38 revolver. Sharples lifted the glass to his lips and found himself peering down at the gun barrel. In a moment of sheer panic, his eyes almost popped out of his head.

'What the bloody...'

Hesketh pulled back the hammer. 'You won't ask me again about the guillotine ever again, Bob. Right?'

He pulled the trigger. Thwack!

Sharples gasped. His face was plastered with theatrical blood.

Cindy, a middle-aged, elfin-like figure, Hesketh's one-time assistant, poured them another glass of champagne. She was a cute and cuddly little thing, like something Hesketh might pull from a top hat in one of his magic shows. They were sitting in a nightclub in town, having just finished their meal.

'But you wouldn't want to marry again, Karl. I mean I wouldn't. Once bitten, twice shy, and all that.'

'Who said anything about marriage? Pulling rabbits out of a hat is one thing but even magicians can't conjure up a happy marriage. No, Cindy, there are limitations to my craft.'

'And us?' she asked demurely.

He raised his glass. 'Togetherness, Cindy. Just you and me.'

She sipped on her champagne in mock celebration. 'And Maggie?'

'I'll take care of that. No problem.'

'And how are you going to take care of *that*?'

He studied her with that matter-of-fact look that was such a hallmark of his stage presentation. 'I'm going to kill her.'

Cindy laughed. 'And pigs might fly.'

He leaned closer to her. 'I'm deadly serious. I'm going to kill her, Cindy.'

Cindy paused and looked long and hard into those great brown eyes of his. 'Blimey, you're serious! But why, Karl? For me? Because I can't think of any other reason. I mean this is preposterous!'

'I'll tell you the reason. After thirty years of marriage, and after having to put up with a woman who drains me of my money, who continuously accuses me of having God knows how many affairs, I feel that enough is enough.'

'But you're in the middle of an affair right now. Come on, Karl, divorce her. It's the cleanest way out and you know it.'

'Oh yes, and she sues me for adultery and I have to stump up. She takes the house, hell knows how much in alimony, and I end up a loser - a tosser! No way, Cindy. Karl Hesketh is a winner,' he ended with great gusto. He drank more champagne. 'Watch.' He lifted the salt cellar from the table and poured some of the salt into his palm. 'Salt, yes?'

Cindy sat up and smiled at him. 'Uh huh.'

'Right.' He emptied the remaining salt into his hand. 'Now, watch.' Next he brought both hands together and began to simulate washing his hands. A moment later he slowly pulled them apart. There was no salt to be seen. 'There. Magic?'

Cindy laughed and took one of his hands in hers. 'Astonishing, Karl. Just how did you do that?'

'That, Cindy, is an example of the wonder of magic. It's that kind of manipulation which will fool even the most intelligent of policemen when they investigate the... what shall I call it? The quite tragic accident of my wife's death.'

Cindy's smile turned sober. 'No, Karl. This is ludicrous. There's no need to... '

'Ah, but it will be a challenge, Cindy. Something to get my teeth into. Now, death by misadventure? Drowning? Poisoning? Electrocution? A car crash? God, there's so many possibilities. I don't know where to start.'

'And I think you're insane, Karl. I think you should pay the bill and take me home,' she declared nonchalantly. She was on her feet. 'I don't think I could ever marry a murderer.'

He spotted a waiter serving at an adjacent table and requested the bill. He too got to his feet.

'Oh, Cindy, come here.'

'What?'

He stretched out a hand and ruffled some of the curls in her black permed hair, then brought his hand in front of her face, 'Your lipstick, madam?'

She laughed again and wrapped her arms around him. 'Oh, Karl, I love you.'

By the time he got home to his country mansion, it was nearing one o'clock in the morning. Maggie was lounging in the television room. She was dressed in a kimono and had a large gin and tonic sitting on the coffee table. There was a musical showing on the television.

She hardly acknowledged his arrival. Continuing to stare at the screen she asked, 'So whose head was it tonight? Male or female? Blonde? Brunette?'

He stood at the door. 'How many drinks tonight? A bottle? Maybe two bottles. I mean it's getting on now, isn't it.'

'My drinking habits are my affair. But you... you just make me sick.'

'I make you sick?' He hung his coat over the door and walked over towards her. 'Look at you. Just look at you. Fifty-two years old, bags under your eyes like potato sacks, and bloodshot with it, hair that looks as though it hasn't been washed in weeks and an ever-expanding mass of fat. Have you no self-respect, woman?'

She turned to him. 'At least I don't go around fucking other men. I might drink a lot but at least I'm faithful to you. Why, I don't know.'

'No man in his right mind would want to fuck a woman who looks like a bloody walrus.' She ignored his words. 'Well, I'm going to bed. I *might* see you in the morning.' He turned on his heel and left.

'If you see that bitch Cindy once more, I promise I'll flippin' kill you!' she shouted. 'I will, I'll kill you!'

She turned back to peer at the television. Hesketh

quietly approached the door. 'Not unless I'm there first - darling.'

It was some time later when Hesketh was conscious of his wife entering the bedroom. Opening an eye, he saw the digital clock numbers on the bedside table; 03:17. There was a clatter as she staggered into the dressing table. It was as if a distillery had just entered the room, such was the smell of alcohol from her breath. He sat motionless and thought. How many more nights was this drunken spare tyre going to disturb his sleep? Weeks? Months? It could go on for years.

There was another thud as she collapsed onto her bed. And he knew that within fifteen minutes the snoring would start. Just like every other night, he closed his eyes and thought about Cindy.

Hesketh was clad in his dressing gown, negotiating his way through a cooked breakfast. He was meditating on the answer to a clue in the *Daily Telegraph* crossword puzzle when Maggie trudged in, her slippers rustling across the parquet flooring.

'Any coffee?' she asked.

'It's in the pot,' Hesketh replied, his attention still fixed to the crossword. She poured herself a black coffee, lit a cigarette and sat down at the table.

'Well then?'

'What?'

'You're no doubt disgusted with me. I mean last night.'

He looked up at her, into those bloodshot eyes.

'Disgusted with you? I've lost count of the number of times I've told you that. Disgusted? No, Maggie. Not disgusted. I'm beyond that now. I feel very, very sorry for you. There was a time when I had much respect for you. For your voice, the way you could hold an operatic audience, when you actually looked after your splendid figure. But now?'

'Did I say anything stupid last night, Karl? Did I? You must tell me. Please.'

'You really want to know, Maggie?'

The hand holding the cigarette shook visibly. 'Yes, yes. I... I was drunk. People say daft things when they're drunk.'

'Okay. You told me you were going to kill me.'

'Never! You're making it up. Putting words into my mouth. I would never do such a thing.'

Hesketh said resolutely, 'Oh yes you did. And the pathetic thing about your outburst is that I believe you.'

She stubbed out the cigarette. 'It's that girl. That's what's causing this. It's her.'

Hesketh rose and took the plate over to the sink. 'I must go now. I have a busy day ahead of me.'

She turned to him, almost pleading. 'Please, Karl, please say you won't see her again. Please. Look, I'll change. No more booze. Honest. I'll stop drinking. I'll go on a diet. I'll get into shape, start looking after myself again. Oh, Karl, please, please!'

'The show starts at eight-thirty. If you're sober, why don't you come along? You'll be most welcome,' he ended with a wry smile.

'Yes, Karl. Yes, I'll do that. That'll be great - so fine!'

'Good, now I must go.'

By late afternoon Maggie had already done the ironing, polished every item of furniture in the house, hoovered the carpets and polished all the windows, inside and out. And for the first time in months she actually felt better, fitter, clearer in the head. She felt an injection of pride in herself that surprised her. The last room to get the treatment was her husband's study, and she almost skipped into the room. She recalled his stating on many occasion that this was his sanctuary, that ultra-personal, little hideaway where many of his magic stunts were invented. And it was sheer coincidence that when she had been cleaning the bedside cabinet earlier in the day she had found the key to the room on the floor next to the cabinet. While she was doing the housework she considered actually going into the study, just to have a look around. Of course, should he return to the house and find her in there, all hell would break loose.

Had she actually said to him that she would kill him if he continued to see that woman? Maybe he had made that up. As she had declared to him in the morning, when you're drunk, you are capable of saying anything - doing anything.

She was at the door of the study. The large mahogany door opened effortlessly and within a moment she was inside. There was a fusty smell about the place which was largely caused by the stacks of books packed into ancient bookcases. More books, papers and magazines lay strewn over tables and chairs, many of them open.

She walked into the centre of the room and looked about the place. It must be seven years since she had last been in here. There were all sorts of contraptions, mainly props he had used in previous magic shows: top hats, magic wands, dolls, bottles and decanters, large playing cards, balls of every size and colour, streamers, cartons of confetti. She sat down at his writing bureau. There were heaps of correspondence, scribbled notes, thumbnail sketches and...

A blueprint of the guillotine.

She switched on the Anglepoise lamp and arranged the blueprint under it to get a better view. It showed the guillotine in plan and side elevations. She then noted another drawing, an isometric drawing, which outlined how the guillotine would work in its 'safety' and 'live' modes. She was taken aback at the simplicity of the construction. It also showed the blade - a twin arrangement, one blade complete and solid, the other having a hemispherical cut-out, obviously used during the 'safety' mode to accommodate the neck of the 'victim'. But the heads in his shows were severed. This wasn't clear from the blueprints. This was the ultimate secret of this particular illusion.

There was a pile of letters open to the side of the drawings, and next to those a list of names. The names corresponded with those on the letters. She scanned the first, picked up a second, a third, a fourth. She began to laugh and chuckle to herself. It was so hilariously obvious that her laughter broke into howls of delight. She just could not help herself from laughing, but she tried hard to compose herself. There was great potential here, she thought. The library in town had a photocopier. It would only take twenty minutes at the most to get there, have the copies done and get back to the house. Okay, let's do it, she thought. She carefully cleared up the letters and the list of names and stuck them into a large manilla envelope.

It was then that the picture came into full view. It was propped up inside one of the compartments in the writing bureau. She lifted it out and put it under the lamp.

Cindy Chesterton. It was a colour head and shoulders shot and, by the squint in her left eye, taken on a sunny day - but by whom?

That was enough. 'Thanks for the invitation, darling,' she said to herself. 'I'll definitely see you later.'

Maggie Hesketh took her seat at the back of the stalls. Her head felt giddy, due in part to the earlier consumption of six gins and tonic. Inside her handbag was a hip flask filled to the brim with neat vodka. That might come in handy later. Earlier in the day she had promised herself that there'd be no more booze, but discovering that photo had finally made her crack.

Yet tonight she was in control, the booze seemingly strengthening her spirit, rather than depressing it. The lights were still on in the auditorium and there was an anticipatory buzz about the place. According to the billboard outside, this was the last evening of the Karl Hesketh Magic Forum, along with the usual grotesque splash about the *Guillotine of Gareth.*

Backstage, Cindy and Hesketh were half-way through a bottle of Dom Perignon '53. He puffed on a fat Romeo and Juliet corona. Tonight she would watch the show from the side of the stage. It would be the first time in months she attended one of his shows. She was so excited.

He was straightening his bow-tie. 'Ah, I feel so good tonight, Cindy. Life is so good, so vibrant, so nourishing. Alas, it is soured by her, but not for long. You see, I have invited her here tonight. I know exactly what I have to do. Soon, very soon, it will be over.'

'No, Karl. Please. This is insane. It will never work. Please, Karl. Just divorce her. It's the easiest way out. You must know that.'

'That's exactly why I am not taking the easy way out.'

There was a knock on the door. A voice said, 'Mr Hesketh, two minutes please.'

'Right,' Hesketh continued, 'how do I look?'

Cindy looked up at him, her face drawn, her brow furrowed. 'You look wonderful, Karl. But I'm afraid you are making a big mistake.'

'Just wait and see, Cindy.'

The orchestra was already playing the introduction. He stubbed out the half-finished cigar, wrapped the large black silk cape around his shoulders and left. The orchestra conductor noted Hesketh's appearance at the side of the stage and led his musicians into a brisk rendering of Tchaikovsky's *Dance of the Sugar Plum Fairy* from *The Nutcracker Suite*. As the lights flooded the stage and the highly acclaimed magician strolled onto it, the audience began applauding, cheering and whistling.

Maggie sat quiet and unmoved. She took a sip from her hip-flask. He began his repertoire by eating an apple and went on to pulling strands and strands of multi-coloured streamers from his mouth. Then the usual series of rope tricks, newspaper cutting and folding illusions, other tricks involving conjuring cutlery, crockery and a complete dining table from nowhere, and the sequel to the Big One; pushing a sabre through his stomach until it appeared through his back. That, as always, brought the audience to its feet.

Throughout the past hour Hesketh said nothing, preferring the silence from his own lips to induce the mysterious air which was so crucial to the finale. Two stage hands walked onto the stage and cleared away all the props he'd used. Meanwhile the curtains closed behind him. He walked slowly over to the front of the stage.

'Ladies and gentlemen,' he began, 'I thank you for your kindness. But I must also warn you that what you are about to witness is not for the faint-hearted.' His voice was as cold as steel and monotone, his body staying motionless, his eyes focusing straight ahead, on nothing in particular. He continued from his now well-prepared speech.

'The guillotine was France's sole means of capital punishment until recent times. Strangely enough, it was the most efficient form of summary justice, leaving nothing to chance, unlike hanging, the electric chair or the gas chamber. Some wretched souls in the past have survived the gallows, others have walked away from the electric chair and in some cases, the gas used in the notorious chamber has not been sufficient to take the life of the victim. Tonight, however, you are going to see someone - one of you - have their head removed.'

People began to whisper and murmur to themselves. Others swallowed nervously. This was the reaction intended. Hesketh continued. 'But alas, it is only magic, my friends. Pure illusion. Whoever dices with death tonight, will return, I hope, to spend a comfortable night's sleep in his - or her - own home.'

At that point the curtains opened. Hesketh nodded to the conductor, who immediately led the orchestra into Ravel's haunting *Bolero*. The stage, all of a sudden, was swathed in dry ice, the smoke wafting around the guillotine which, by now, was firmly in place at the centre of the stage. The lights were dimmed to a rosy iridescence. Hesketh went over to inspect it and, from behind, removed a large water melon. This he placed on the head block. He glanced up at the blade and placed his hand on the lever. He turned to look at the audience in a defiant manner, pulled the lever, the blade thundered down and in an instant the water melon was cleanly halved in two. He lifted both halves of the fruit and took them over to show them to the audience. Then he dried his hands with a handkerchief. The music toned down a little.

'Right now, ladies and gentlemen, I am going to ask one of the theatre audience to volunteer - what should I say, their service - to the greater cause of magic.'

People in the audience looked at each other, some tittering, whilst others sat firmly in their seats. Hesketh looked over to one side of the aisle as if to ask someone in particular, when a voice was heard from the rear of the stalls. It was Maggie. She had just returned the hip flask to her handbag and was on her feet and making her way down to the stage. Hesketh smiled.

'Ah, ladies and gentlemen, we have a brave member of the public. Please give her a warm round of applause.'

At first people clapped, then they cheered, and the applause grew stronger. Someone was either very brave indeed or a complete idiot. At least that was how it appeared to the thousand or so people in the audience.

Maggie stepped onto the stage to much cheering. She took one long look at her husband and then an equally long stare at the guillotine. Somehow it seemed more evil, more formidable and dangerous than it did on a piece of paper.

'So you managed it, my dear,' Hesketh whispered to her.

'I wouldn't miss it for the world,' came Maggie's reply.

The clapping died down, and again Hesketh commanded quietness. Very softly, the orchestra continued the *Bolero*.

'Ladies and gentlemen, you have witnessed what the guillotine does to a simple water melon. I should inform you that the blade itself weighs fifty pounds, is razor sharp and has a drop of fifteen feet. This guillotine, in practice, has sheared the body of a dead sheep in one swoop. That is an indication of the force acting on the head block, as you see here. And now this kind lady is going to undertake the experiment. We all wish her well.'

'You're fucking crazy!' hissed Maggie. 'I know how this thing works and when you're through I'm gonna tell the whole world about your stupid magic illusion.'

Hesketh could smell the alcohol on her breath. He whispered, 'No, my darling, it is you who are fucking stupid!'

When Hesketh had cut the water melon in half, he had adjusted the lever to the 'live' position. Normally, this would be changed to the 'safety' mode when it came to the severed head part of the act, and the volunteer from the audience. But it would be no illusion this time. His wife had turned up unexpectedly; what a turn in his fortunes. This would be a tragic accident, a magic trick that went seriously wrong. He would, he suddenly convinced himself, get off with a manslaughter charge. Excellent!

However, Maggie knew the secret of the machine. It did not actually lie in the construction of the machine itself, but in the people selected for the illusion. She had walked calmly around the guillotine and discreetly slipped the adjusting knob to the 'safety' mode.

Hesketh went through the actions of helping Maggie kneel in the right position, manipulating her head on the block. Everything was in place. Hesketh nodded to the conductor, who phased out the music and phased in the timpani drum. More dry ice appeared around the guillotine. His hand was on the lever. Then the timpani rolled ever and ever more louder, the spotlight focused on the head...

'Goodbye my love. Goodbye and good riddance!' He pulled the lever.

Swish!

The blade swooped down. The lights were killed. Cindy looked on in amazement from the side of the stage. There were screams from some sections of the audience.

As the lights came on and the dry ice cleared, Hesketh couldn't believe his eyes. Gasps of relief issued from the audience, and then wave upon wave of applause. Hesketh had to think on his feet. What had gone wrong?

He retracted the blade and allowed Maggie to rise from the guillotine unscathed. As she did so she turned to the audience.

'Ladies and gentlemen, as you can see I have survived the punishment which Karl Hesketh stated earlier was impossible. What about if he, the magician, were to put his head on the chopping block?' That brought some tense laughter from the audience. 'What would happen then?' It was as if the audience figured that maybe this was part of the show. 'What do you say, ladies and gentlemen?'

There were yells to the affirmative. Hesketh looked at Maggie and smiled obstinately. What was happening? What had gone wrong? And the severed head? What was the audience thinking? But he had to play to his audience. They came first. So he let her continue. After all, the mechanism was on the 'safety' mode.

Things had changed. Now he had *his* head on the block. The stage hands looked bemusedly at each other and hurriedly flooded the stage with dry ice again. The orchestra began to play, then the phasing of the music and the roll of the timpani drum.

She had her hand on the lever as she whispered, 'Well, Karl, have you any last wishes?'

Hesketh managed to turn his head a little and squinted up at her. 'What are you talking about?'

'Oh I know how this contraption works all right. I found the plans in your study today, the picture of that bitch, Cindy Chesterton. Oh, and the names of the people who you seemingly picked from the audience at random. And then there's the severed heads. That must have cost a fortune having all those people's heads reproduced. And yes, my darling, I know all about the safe and live modes of this contraption.'

Maggie turned her head to the audience with a defiant grin on her lips and the hand on the level.

Hesketh's brow was by now lashing with sweat. 'Look,' he began, his voice barely audible above the roll of the timpani drum, 'for God's sake, Maggie, don't be stupid. This thing can kill! Now let me out of here,' he pleaded.

'Sorry, Karl, but the audience have paid good money. They're looking for action. And guess what, the police will see it as an unfortunate accident. And you know what, Karl, I reckon I'll get off with manslaughter.'

Swish! Chunk!

Me Today, You Tomorrow

The old man lay in repose, propped up against a shop window, literally four feet away from the gutter. His eyes were fixed on the torrent of rainwater which hurried past him, seemingly oblivious of the rain which pelted down on his long, matted locks. The cardboard 'bed' was sodden through and through and it was just as well that he was wrapped up in the ex-army trench coat and hobnail boots, not that they provided much comfort from the elements.

He took another mouthful of Carlberg's Special Brew from the can and wiped his mustachioed mouth dry - well, as dry as the weather would allow. He was facing yet another lonely night in this soulless city.

He looked down at his cloth cap. There was maybe ninety pence in total. That wouldn't even buy him another beer.

He was about to lift the cap when he heard footsteps

approaching him. The footsteps belonged to a man in a pin-striped suit huddled under an umbrella. The old man quickly lifted the cap and held it out with much expectation. He gazed up at the pin-stripes.

'A few pennies for an old man, mister?'

The man stopped and looked down into two soulful, watery eyes. 'You'll catch your death on a night like this old man.'

'Just a few coins, mister. That's all.'

The man looked at the Carlsberg. 'For a drink?'

'I'm not an alcoholic, sir. I'm a human being,' he replied in a dignified voice, a voice which certainly did not match the old man's seemingly destitute situation.

'I assume you are homeless?'

'My home is where my heart is, sir.' He coughed and spluttered. 'And your home, sir? Looking at you I would proffer that you live in a very large house. You're a businessman, successful with it, happily married.' The old man stroked his beard. 'Let's see. You'll be about forty-five, maybe have two kids... '

The man smiled. In fact it was the first time today that a smile had breached his lips.

'Okay, okay, okay. Enough is enough. Here,' he said, handing the old man a five pound note, 'that'll buy you at least three Carlsbergs and a packet of cheese and onion, but maybe you should go and buy yourself a nice warm meal somewhere.'

'Thank you, sir,' the old man replied. 'And your name, sir?'

'I don't think it matters in the least. But it's Jeremy. Jeremy Wellington.'

The old man extended a hand. 'No relation to the Duke?' he asked happily.

'No. No relation to the Duke.'

They shook hands. 'And you?'

'What's that, sir?'

'Your name?'

'Maximilian Wesley. You can call me Max, sir.'

Wellington laughed. That was a smile *and* a laugh, and both in one day as well. 'Oh, come on, pull the other leg. Maximilian Wesley? Never. John Smith, yes.'

Wesley drained the remaining drops from the can. He got to his feet. 'You know, sir, nobody believes my name. It was the one I was born with, nevertheless. But because of my impoverishment and penurious circumstances, people in general never believe me. However, Mr Jeremy Wellington, perhaps it will be a matter of *hodie mihi, cras tibi!*'

Wellington regarded the old man with growing wonderment. 'What?'

The old tramp was already on his way. He stopped several yards down the wet pavement and turned to Wellington. He translated, 'Me today, you tomorrow!'

Wellington and his wife Judy were drinking coffee in the lounge of their town house. The house was perhaps a mile from where he had met the old man earlier in the evening. Judy was forty years old, a plain sort of woman, freckly-faced and frail, but a dedicated mother and music teacher.

Soft classical music played in the background. 'So it's a matter of cutbacks then?' Judy said.

Wellington had a folder opened on his knee. 'There's nothing for it. I had Tony double-check the figures for the last quarter's trading. It doesn't look good, Judy. In fact I'll have to lay off at least ten, maybe fifteen.'

'As many as that?'

'I'm afraid so.'

'But the Italian order. Have they stopped buying British suits nowadays?'

'Selling suits to the Italians is like selling sand to the Arabs. No. Things are looking bad, Judy, and if the American contract doesn't materialise next month, then I think... '

'What?'

'Never mind.'

Wellington put away the folder and took off his reading glasses. He sighed heavily and stretched his arms. 'I think it was Macmillan who said 'We've never had it so good'. I came across an old chap tonight. A right old tramp he was. Lying there on the pavement, drinking a Carlsberg Special lager, and quite stinking he was. And you know, Judy, for a minute or two I could've swapped places with him.'

'Nonsense, Jeremy. Absolute claptrap. What are you talking about? A tramp?'

'Yeah, you know. They walk about the streets like scarecrows. Invariably drunk, probably steal whatever they can get their hands on and usually end up in a fight. Then it's off to the police cell for the night. But this chap was certainly different.'

'Perhaps you were seeing things, dear. The state the business is in. You know. That kind of thing.'

'No, this chap... well I couldn't put my finger on it. Strange, really. And he spoke in perfect Queen's English.'

'Well I think we should be going to bed. You've had a long hard day. Golf tomorrow?'

'No. I'm meeting Tony tomorrow in the office. We're going over some plans on a loan scheme and a scenario to streamline the business. Time is running short.'

'A nightcap, then?'

'Yes. A large Cognac.'

It was midday. The office looked as though a bomb had hit it. Tony, the company accountant, a lean, athletic figure with thin straight gingerish hair and a hooked nose, sat at his laptop. Wellington was sitting at an adjacent desk, wading through company accounts and trading bills. Even the floor was covered in neat piles of paper and stacks of files lay beside the filing cabinets.

Tony keyed in some figures into his laptop and turned to his boss. 'Nope. Shit, no matter what figures I enter, it keeps coming up with the same old story.'

Wellington wheeled over in his chair and peered into the laptop screen. 'Which is?'

'We're a million and a half in the red, Jeremy, and if we project future business trends based on the last quarter, it could lead to serious problems.' Tony slumped back into his chair.

'But Barclays? The loan? I thought a deal was in the offing?'

'They would laugh in our faces. I think we'll have to wait and see what the New York contract offers us. If J.J. Samuels don't come up with the business, then I'm afraid... '

'It's as bad as that?'

'No amount of borrowing will help. Yesterday, I thought we had enough assets on which to base a short-term loan. But the interest rates would crucify us. It would lead to bankruptcy.'

Wellington looked like a punch-drunk boxer. He had taken it on the chin, but somehow he was not about to come out for the next round. If he threw the towel in now he could cut his losses and run; perhaps go back to accountancy. He always had that to fall back on. But he couldn't. Over the past fifteen years the success of his clothing company had furnished him with the wherewithal to purchase a town house, right in the centre of the city, the Aston Martin, a yacht moored on the Thames. Most of the furniture in his house was Edwardian antiques. His personal assets were approaching half a million.

'What about, as we said yesterday, paying off some of the staff? Would that help, Tony?'

'I suppose so but we're in a Gordian Knot situation. Pay off half the staff, then you don't have the hands to tackle the American job. Keep them and you're postponing the inevitable. The American contract, if we get it, would only allow for a small reduction in a rather unwieldy overdraft.'

Wellington placed his head in his hands. 'Damn it!'

After a moment's reflection he asked, 'Well, Tony, as they would say in the States, what's the bottom line?'

Tony switched off the laptop, as if that act alone signalled the inevitable. 'Cut your losses, Jeremy. Sell up. You might just cover your losses. But what with redundancies, bank charges, VAT, etc...'

Wellington took a long hard look at Tony, a modern day Pontius Pilate. 'Fancy a drink?'

'The Three Maidens?'

'Let's do it.'

Having got quite drunk, they left the Three Maidens close to midnight. Tony jumped into a taxi and Jeremy decided to walk home, although it turned into more of a stagger. He couldn't remember when he had last had such a good old binge, although he did know he had come out of the pub with not a penny in his wallet. But he felt happy. Booze had that wonderful temporary effect of erasing from the memory the sharp edges of life, smoothing away the lumps and bumps, of everyday hang-ups. He wondered how the old man, Max, got by on a day-to-day basis, being loaded all the time. His memory would be all but a blank television screen by now.

A hundred yards along the street he could ask the question, because the old man lay in a shop doorway. It was the same street in which he had encountered him two or three days before.

Wellington stopped and bent down for a closer look. 'It's you, isn't it?' he asked in the semi-darkness.

The old man's face looked more drawn, more grimy than

the last time. 'Mr Jeremy Wellington, I presume,' he joked in that perfect diction.

'And you're... eh, Max. Maximilian...' Then he burped. 'Maximilian. No, I can't remember your last name.'

'Is John Smith easier to remember, my friend?'

'I'll stick with Max. Anyway, how are you? Are you pissed tonight, Max? Because I'm pissed tonight. Really pissed - in fact pissed off as well.'

Max took a couple of cans of beer from the pocket of his trench coat. 'Let's drink to the collective weaknesses of the human race, Mr Wellington. Or can I call such a fine gentleman as yourself by your Christian name?'

Wellington took the can and pulled the ring-pull. 'I'll drink to that, Max. In fact I'd drink to anything tonight. Let's drink a toast to freedom. Freedom from money, taxmen, insurance policies, bills and the dreaded VAT. By the way, yes, you can call me Jeremy.'

Max laughed. His teeth, at least the ones still remaining in his mouth, were tarnished and stained. Then he coughed. It was hoarse and rasping. 'Excuse me, Jeremy. Bronchitis, you know. A sad reflection on this miserable existence of mine. You are what you make of yourself. Look at me. A down-and-out with no possessions, no future, no life. But you? You have everything diametrically opposed to me. Contradistinction, if you will.'

Wellington sat down beside the strange old codger. 'You have a way with words, Max. Somewhere away down deep inside that skull of yours is a hidden person. Yes, Max, there's a deeper side to you. You're not the drunken tramp one sees on television dramas. So come on. Cut out the bullshit. Who are you?'

Max laughed again. This time it was a real belly laugh. However, it had the effect of bringing on another bout of coughing.

'Life, Jeremy, is a long three-act tragedy. All emotions are contained within the script: pain, agony, joy, love, heartache, ecstasy, melancholy. I've been to all those places. Some of them it's been my misfortune to visit on more than a thousand occasions. Right now my day is filled working with the scene called 'Misery'. And it is a scene that seems to have no reasonable end in sight. It's ghastly.'

'Hah! Caught you. That is of your own doing. Life isn't that hard that someone should end up like you. Look at you, Max. Dressed in stinking old clothes; you probably haven't had a shave in years, your hair's dishevelled, your hands are scaly and dirty. Have you no self-respect? None? Shit, my next door neighbour's spaniel is cleaner than you.'

Max found this all very funny. He chuckled with a self-assertiveness which caught Wellington off guard.

'Jeremy, let me tell you something. I learnt a very long time ago to give up the ghost of ambition. It haunted me for ten years before I eventually had it exorcised. I suppose it was the failure I couldn't cope with, the feeling that the sum total of all one's efforts and aspirations had added up to nought. Quite frightening. But I am forever looking over my shoulder at fear.'

'Oh is that right now?' Wellington asked. 'I know something, Max, being in your position would drive me to suicide. I'd kill myself. I would. I would. I'd bloody kill myself. But you? That's the question. How have you, a fine man in his earlier days, I bet, ended up here, like this?'

'Me? A long story, my friend.' He supped more of the lager. 'You see I lost my wife when I was 40 years old. Let me see now. That'd be nearly 30 years ago now. I ran a corner shop. You know the type of things: groceries, vegetables, ironmongery, soap powder, fags - everything under the sun. But they opened up one of those supermarkets, didn't they, and within a year I had to sell up. But I always fancied myself as a playwright. Back in those days we would go to the theatre at least once a month, me and Joyce. Wonderful, charming evenings they were. But she left me. The Lord himself took her away. The only therapy open to me was in my writing. I must have written twenty-five plays in three years and you know, Jeremy, not one of them was produced. I remember the rejection slips. They came in through the letterbox like death sentences, cruel and vicious, like poison pen letters.

'It was then that I started to drink. In the beginning it was a half-bottle a day and near the end it was getting on for two bottles. I started selling my possessions and got myself into debt. Selling my typewriter signified the beginning of the end. I eventually got jailed for breaking into a post office. When they let me out I began picking pockets, stealing from those horrid supermarkets, but once more I ended up in jail. For the past ten years I have been a nomad, wandering in circles, killing time, courting misfortune. Believe me, Jeremy, don't get encumbered with ambition or you might just end up like me.'

'I'd love to read one of your plays though. Perhaps I would learn more about you,' Wellington said encouragingly.

'Very well deduced, my friend.'

'I suppose you scrapped them all, anyway. I think that would be my reaction.'

'Not at all. I believe my sister, Margaret, still has them. Mind you, I haven't seen her for nearly ten years now. She moved to Edinburgh. That's if she's still alive.'

'Look,' Wellington said, taking his wallet and pen from his jacket, 'give me her address. I'll take you up to Edinburgh. Both of us. What do you say?'

'Why all this interest, Jeremy? I'm an old man who neither seeks fame and certainly nor fortune. It's a bit late in the day for that. No, I'm like an old piece of driftwood which gets washed up on the seashore. I am as nondescript as one of my plays. So let's forget it, eh?'

'I'd still like to read your work.'

Max regarded the stranger with a smile. 'Okay, if you so wish. Now, let me see. Uh, yes, it's fifty-nine Alexander Street, somewhere near the city centre if my memory serves me well.'

Wellington wrote the address down on the back of one of his business cards. He returned the card to his wallet.

'Look I'm not doing anything next weekend. I'll take you up. Of course you cannot go in those rags. But I'll get you some clothes, shoes, and, by the way, a visit to the barber's won't go amiss. So what do you think, old man?'

'You don't give up easily, do you? No, I think I'll stay here. By the weekend I might be dead. Who knows?'

Wellington shook his head, got to his feet and finished the can of beer. He wrapped the collar of his jacket tight around his neck.

'Next Saturday, Max. Have we got a deal?'

'You take care of your business, Jeremy, and I'll take care of mine.'

Wellington took one last look at the old tramp and hurried away down the street.

It was Thursday morning. Wellington and his accountant, Tony, sat staring at the telephone. The news had come as a shattering blow; the American contract had gone to one of their competitors. It was the final nail in the coffin. They had already contacted the liquidators who would arrive the following week to handle the company's financial situation and formally place it in administration.

Wellington could only sit back and wonder as to the rapidity of it all. These faceless men in grey suits and narrow ties had arrived in the morning, cleared the offices of all files and computer records and were gone by the afternoon.

Two days later he received a letter stating the particulars of the bankruptcy and a solitary figure of the actual amount owing to the liquidators: £1,900,000. Even with the sale of his house and other personal assets, he reckoned he might have enough to buy a small flat or cottage. But that was all.

The following two weeks' events passed terminally quickly for Jeremy Wellington as he and his wife sat in the kitchen for the last time. They were sitting on two large cardboard boxes drinking coffee.

'The place looks so barren, Jeremy. Just the other week I was cooking Venetian liver and onions in this quaint old kitchen.' She stopped to wrap up a cup in an old newspaper.

'Well, tomorrow we'll be in our own little flat. At least it'll be a roof over our heads. It could be a lot worse, Judy.'

'I still can't believe this has all happened. One day we seem to have everything and the next...'

Wellington stretched out his arms and gave her a warm embrace. She was almost in tears. What woman wouldn't be?

'Come, come, Judy. All's not lost. There'll be better times. I promise. We'll rise above all this. You wait and see.'

She looked up into his eyes. 'I'll always love you, Jeremy, even if we don't have a penny.'

They began wrapping up the remaining cups and saucers before tackling the pots, pans and cutlery.

'Right then,' Wellington said, 'let's finish off this lot.'

There was a stack of newspapers and magazines on the draining board by the sink which he divided into two piles.

'Okay, one lot for you and one lot for me.'

The first newspaper he lifted was a recent edition of the *Evening Gazette*. He glanced over the front page in an extemporaneous manner, his eye not looking for anything in particular. But there was something several lines long tucked away down in the bottom right hand corner. The caption read: TRAMP FOUND DEAD ON CITY STREET.

His eye traversed the copy. 'Oh my God!' he exclaimed.

Judy turned around. 'Yes, darling? What's up?'

'This here. It's that old tramp. What was his name again? I think it was Max.'

'Who's Max?'

'It must be him. He was found dead, according to this, two weeks ago on St George's Street. Seems the shopkeeper found him. It must be him!'

'So! What about him? Who? What's so special?' Judy asked.

'Don't you see? It must be him, the playwright, Judy. A very articulate man he was, and certainly no ordinary tramp.' He put down the newspaper. 'Now where's my wallet?'

Wellington got to his feet and went through to the hall.

'Jeremy, would you mind telling me what this is all about?' He returned a moment later with his wallet.

'Now, I think I put it in here.' He took out one of his business cards. 'Here it is. Right. Fifty-nine, Alexander Street, Edinburgh.'

'Jeremy, please!' It was more of a protest.

'It's a long story, Judy. But I'll be going up to Edinburgh on Saturday.'

It had been raining all the way up on the train but by the time Wellington reached Waverley Station, Edinburgh, the rain had subsided into a drizzle. He was armed with a street map and umbrella and was already crossing Princess Street, the famous shopping thoroughfare of the capital city. Then it was down Leith Walk, heading towards the docks; he figured Alexander Street was about a half-mile down on the left. Within ten minutes he was turning into it, a cobbled road flanked on either side by dreary tenement blocks.

Number 59 was the top flat in the block. Well-trodden, winding stairs led him to the door. It was a dank and dismal setting, just like the weather outside. Had Maximilian Wesley once lived here? He rapped three times on the heavy brass door knocker.

The door opened slowly to reveal a small, toothless face, wrinkled and grey.

'Hello,' Wellington said tentatively, 'Margaret? Margaret Wesley?'

'No,' the voice croaked. 'My name is Margaret Smith.' The voice was frail and almost inaudible.

'But you are the brother of Max, Maximilian Wesley?'

'What do ye want?'

'Can I come in please? I need to talk to you. It's important.'

She opened the door and allowed Wellington inside, leading him into a small sitting room which was chock-a-block with antique furniture. A coal fire was ablaze, which brought a welcoming comfort to Wellington's sodden feet. The old lady gestured to a rocking chair by the side of the fireplace. She took a chair on the other side.

'My name is Jeremy Wellington, Mrs Smith. I have some bad news for you. Your brother, Max, I met several weeks ago. He was living the life of a... homeless person. He gave me your address. I'm afraid he's dead. I read it in a newspaper down south.' He came to an abrupt halt to gauge the reaction. There was none. He continued. 'He was a very kind man and intelligent. I'd like to have known him better. Did he ever come to visit you, Mrs Smith?'

'Visit me? Never. It must be well over ten years now, Mr Wellington. But his death disnae surprise me, ye ken. No, he was a loner most o' his life after his wife died. He worshipped Joyce, adored her. Then he turned his hand to writing. Max would spend hour upon hour in his study.' She smiled. 'Aye, I still read his plays from time to time. However, if the auld bugger's dead then so be it. But it is sad, very sad.' She paused for a moment. 'Would ye like a cup o' tea, Mr Wellington?'

'Yes, in a minute.' He wasn't sure how to approach the next subject. He believed the scripts might be stored away in some vault, or in some dark corner of an attic. 'Look, Mrs Smith, it would please me enormously to read some of your brother's work. I feel I'd learn more about him in his plays. Would that be possible?'

'Of course, be my guest. Most o' the time they sit in a cupboard gathering dust.'

She got to her feet. For a woman Wellington thought would be in her early eighties, she was quite sprightly on her feet. Wellington followed her into the bedroom, where she opened a wall cupboard door; one of the manuscripts fell from a pile and onto the floor. The manuscripts were stacked at various angles and almost took up the whole of the cupboard.

'There's a spare room next door with a table and chair. Ye can read them through there if you like.'

'I'd love that, Mrs Smith.'

'Right, I'll away and put on the kettle.'

At nine o'clock in the evening Wellington was still engrossed in reading. The scripts themselves, numbering twenty-four, were partly hand-written, partly typed. The plays were interspersed with notes on character studies, stage designs, costumes ideas, even lighting arrangements. Some of the scenes Wellington thought hilarious, others tragic. The style and strength of the dialogue could have been penned by Shakespeare himself. And all of this from some tramp he had accidentally bumped into a couple of months ago. It had not taken him long to realise that he was in possession of something extraordinary special.

He leaned back in the chair and opened up another script, this one entitled *All Men Are Beasts*. Then the door opened.

'Mr Wellington, it has just gone nine o'clock. Did you drive here?'

Wellington glanced at his watch. 'Shit! Ooops. Excuse me, Mrs Smith. I didn't think it was so late. My train was leaving at nine-thirty.'

'Ye can stay here if you want. I think I've an old sleeping bag in the bedroom.'

He smiled at the old lady. 'That is very kind of you, Mrs Smith. Yes I will. By the way, these plays of Max are quite astonishing. The whole world needs to see them.'

'Aye, Mr Wellington, I thought ye might like them. They're very good. Max always had a way with words.'

'Yes, I understand that perfectly now.'

By seven o'clock the next morning, Wellington had read them all, and it was then that he thought of Judy. She would be worrying over his whereabouts. Not to worry. He recalled earlier leaving his mobile at home but, not to worry, he would phone her from the railway station. Meantime it was a matter of getting washed and maybe a cup of tea.

Mrs Smith was up and about by eight. Wellington entered the kitchen, where the old lady was preparing toast.

'Good morning, Mrs Smith, and how are we this morning?'

'Ah, Mr Wellington. Are ye leaving now?' she asked.

'Yes. My wife will be wondering what's happened to me.' She continued to butter the toast and pour a cup of tea.

'Mrs Smith, I hope you will pardon me for being a bit forward and that, but I have a favour to ask of you.'

'Go ahead, Mr Wellington.' She sat down at the dining table.

'I would be honoured if I could take one of Max's plays away with me. You see my wife has contacts in the theatrical world. I'm sure these plays would be successful. I mean they're brilliant pieces of work. What do you think? Of course there'd be money in it for you.'

'At my age, Mr Wellington, the money woudnae interest me.' She paused to have a bite of toast. 'But yes, ye can take them.'

'Them, Mrs Smith?' he asked, puzzled.

'Aye, ye can take them all. But I would ask ye one thing, Mr Wellington.'

'And that is?' he asked enthusiastically.

'Will ye keep me informed on what's goin' on?'

'But of course. Absolutely.'

She got to her feet and stepped over to a wall cabinet, from which she withdrew a buff-coloured envelope. 'Here, Mr Wellington, take these. They're pictures of Max during happier times.'

Wellington took the envelope and extracted the photographs.

'I'll go and find some carrier bags for the plays,' she said.

Judy picked up her husband from the station later that day. He made his apologies for the previous evening, only to be told of a letter that had arrived from his solicitors whilst he was in Edinburgh. The liquidators who had wrapped up his business were demanding over a hundred thousand pounds for interest in bankers' loans. But he did not have that kind of money. They would have to wait, he said.

Later that evening Wellington had his wife read through a couple of the plays, anything to take their minds of their predicament. She, like her husband, was awestruck by the genius of the writing and wasted no time in phoning Donald Batty, a theatre agent and close friend. Yes, he would love to read them and, within a couple of days, he had done so.

Within nine months, the first of the plays, *All Men Are Beasts*, appeared in London's West End. Wellington took the trouble to invite Margaret Smith as guest of honour on the opening night. She agreed to entrust Wellington with managing this and any future plays. The old lady had kept her word; she would not want a penny from her brother's success. As it happened, however, Wellington made sure she would not want for the rest of her life. *All Men Are Beasts* became an overnight success, a smash hit in the West End and would be appearing on Broadway within a year. But even before that, two other plays went into rehearsal.

It had been three years since Jeremy Wellington had gone bust. Now a successful producer in his own right, the one-time clothing manufacturer had befriended many stars of stage and screen. Regrettably, Margaret Smith had passed away during this time, but she had shown her appreciation and regard for Wellington by naming him as the sole benefactor of the rights to all Maximilian Wesley's plays. The phone never stopped in his new office, which, ironically, was located in the same street as his defunct clothing business.

He was sitting in his new office with both feet up on the desk. It had just gone six o'clock. 'Yes, Judy,' he said into the phone, 'I'll meet you in the Beefeater at seven. Well it's been a long hard day. Sweat, blood, tears and toil as usual. Uh-huh. You've been looking at another house? Oh, come on. You'll want a world cruise next! So enough of that. Okay, so, the Beefeater at seven? Right. See you there. Bye.'

He made another couple of phone calls.

The Beefeater restaurant was a ten-minute walk from the office and he reckoned he would make it just on time. On the way he would pop into the newsagent and buy a cigar. In recent times he had developed a penchant for cigars; just the thing to finish off a fine meal.

It was a particularly mild evening as he closed the office

door behind him. The traffic roared past him in both directions and even at this time in the evening the streets were quite busy. Just as well he had left the car at home today, as felt like cracking open a bottle of champagne to go with their meal.

He stepped on to the street and began walking at speed, checking his watch as he went. The newsagent's shop was fifty or so yards down on the right. He began quickening his step when, quite out of the blue, he tripped over a pair of boots, almost landing flat on his face. The man was propped up in the doorway of a shoe shop a couple of doors up from the newsagents.

Wellington got to his feet, at the same time turning around to look at the man. 'Can't you look where you're going?' the voice screamed at him.

Wellington could only stare in bewilderment: the wiry hair, the unkempt beard, large crumpled overcoat, hob-nailed boots, the putrid smell of urine.

He squinted his eyes. 'You can't be. Never. No, that's not possible.'

'What are you havering about? Eh?' It was an angry voice.

Wellington smiled in anticipation, stretching out his hand in the process.

'You're... you're Maximilian Wesley, aren't you?'

'Max who? Sorry guv'nor. Nope. What's it to you anyway?'

'You're not Max? Maximilian Wesley?' he asked in astonishment.

'Huh, will you just listen to you, mister. I'm John Smith, so go on, beat it!'

There's Something in the Air

Wilson Harris stood at the door of the British Airways 737 on the runway at Aberdeen Airport, smiling and breathing fresh air for the first time in years. He wished the hostess goodbye. Just as he reached the bottom of the metal staircase, a large seagull dropping spattered the shoulder of his black leather jacket. To most mortals this would engender pure embarrassment, but to Harris it was wonderful, possibly a mysterious pointer to things greater.

And the colour. It was black, its texture shiny and extremely viscous. Being an occultist, a magician and a mental gymnast, he figured there was a deeper meaning to this event. Black gull shit? Well, what colour is it usually? White? Cream? Grey-green?

Rather than wipe it off, he decided to leave it and instead made his way to the arrivals terminal. A taxi dropped him outside the guest house which would be his lodgings for the duration of his working trip to the city. Harris took another voluminous swig of North East air, so crystalline clear, almost ambrosial in quality, before strolling up the path to the front door.

On a shiny brass plate to the side of the door were the etched words: 'The Dark Friary Bed and Breakfast.' He swallowed anxiously before ringing the door bell and within seconds, a woman's face appeared. It was ashen and thin, wrinkled, the nose hooked and pointed. Her deep-socketed eyes were green, her hair, wiry, grey and straggly. The harelip was so humbling to view.

She croaked slowly, 'You must be Mr Harris.'

'Correct,' he replied, offering his hand. She refused it.

'I have been expecting you.'

She closed the door silently behind him. Her gait showed a pronounced stoop. The place stank of incense; Harris knew it to be sandalwood. The walls were papered with a design of Oriental origin on which were hung several paintings: a Blake here, a Gauguin there. And then it was up a narrow winding staircase to his room. On the way up the dimly-lit staircase he brushed past a black cat. He could hear a snoring sound from one of the adjoining rooms.

'Don't worry about him, Mr Harris,' she said, 'you'll rarely see him.'

'Oh!'

'This is your room, Mr Harris,' she continued, opening the door, which creaked painfully. 'It's not much but it is tidy and quiet. You won't be disturbed. You could die in this place, Mr Harris, and no one would ever know - unless I told them, that is.'

Harris laughed half-heartedly and nervously took the key. 'I certainly won't die of breathing your fine Scottish air,' he replied, in a brogue with just a hint of Cockney running through it.

She paused before leaving and smiled to reveal a set of teeth that resembled a row of derelict houses. 'By the way, Mr Harris, black gull excreta in this part of the world is a sign of the devil.'

Harris stood there, puzzled, and glanced around at his shoulder. The black, slithery shit had disappeared.

He lay on the bed looking up at the ceiling. A solitary lamp illuminated the sparse room. He was conscious of a stale smell which he reckoned was due to the age and state of the furniture. It reminded him of a trip to Dartmoor the previous year, that peaty, fusty odour of the landscape just before dawn. The stentorian incumbent in the next room wheezed and hissed and then snored a raucous, haunting melody. Surely that couldn't be the sound of a human being? But it had continued unabated for three hours now.

Harris took a sip of a vitamin C drink which he had brought with him and closed his eyes. Images of leaving his wife and family. Covent Garden bathed in sunshine. Heathrow Airport, the parting, the airport formalities, the six whiskies on the plane, the forty winks, the relatively turbulent-free flight. And that black gull shit. Where did that fit in? What was the meaning of that? Did it have a meaning? And how did that old witch know about...

The snoring was getting louder. It was as if somebody or something was going through hell. And then specks of rain began peppering the window. Within a few seconds, it increased to a constant downpour. A deep rumble was evident in the distance, followed by a flash of lightning.

Harris sat up, swung his legs over the bed and peered out into the darkness. His face was reflected in the window as a skeletal opaqueness. Another crash of thunder and blanket lightning ensued before the bedside table lamp went dead. He immediately crawled over to the cupboard and picked out a candle. Upon lighting it, he placed it on a saucer and stood it on the bedside table. He lit a cigarette at the same time and decided to listen to the storm raging outside. It felt comfortable to be inside, cosy, warm, the protection from the awful weather suddenly wrapping itself around Kintore. Was this Scotland? Rain, winds, thunderstorms, seagull shit?

He stubbed out his cigarette and began counting the seconds between the thunderclap and the lightning; he knew the storm to be subsiding. It was getting on for ten o'clock and it had been a long day. But how was he to sleep with all that noise from Rip Van Winkle next door?

There was only one thing for it: his MP3 player. After cleaning up and doing his teeth, he put on the headphones, lay down on the bed and listened to a sound effects tape of sheep bleating. Ah, bliss! Unadulterated pleasure.

A beam of light cut through the lace curtains and painted a ghostly image on the linen quilt. Harris woke to the sounds of a natural alarm: snoring. His digital watch told him it was six thirty-seven. This guy through the wall had been sleeping for well on twelve hours!

He had to be at the office by eight, so he decided to get up there and then. Having showered and dressed, he made his way down to the dining room. The cat which he had passed on the stairs the previous night he passed again on the way down. Did the cat have anything to do with the Sleeper?

The dining room was awash with the scent of sandalwood, the room accommodating two tables and chairs. He sat down at the one nearest the window and waited. There were no breakfast smells. No radio was playing. But he could hear the snoring. It seemed to pulsate, radiate through the ceiling, down the walls, along the floorboards, up the table legs. Christ, who was this guy?

Mrs Witch appeared from a small door along from the window. She was clad in a black lace shawl and grey velvet dress. A pair of pince-nez straddled her nose.

'You'd like breakfast, Mr Harris?'

'Eh, yes... I think,' he replied. And then, 'By the way, I didn't catch your name last night.'

'Names, Mr Harris? Appelations? Do they really matter?'

'No, but I thought... '

'It's Wyche, Mr Harris, Evelyn Wyche.'

Harris almost slid off his chair.

'I see.' This was weird, he thought to himself. Time for a change of subject. 'Uh, could I have some orange juice, please, Mrs Wyche?'

'Sorry, I only have tomato juice. Of course you could have some black coffee. I do like red and black, y'know what I mean?'

No, he didn't. Well, he did but...

'You'll want black pudding, Mr Harris. You just love black pudding. Isn't that right?'

Harris cleared his throat. 'Eh, funnily enough, yes, but...'

'It's the blood in black pudding, Mr Harris, isn't it? My black pudding is the best in the whole of Scotland. You see it's the type of blood one uses.'

'I don't doubt it.'

'Of course I always serve liver as well. Nice and raw. That's how they all like it. Believe me.'

'Yeah, but... '

'And eggs, Mr Harris, you'll have eggs, no doubt.'

'Love 'em, yeah.'

'Good. I always serve them scrambled of course, with just a little smidgeon of tarragon. Absolutely delicious. You'll think this a bit zany, no?'

'No, Mrs... eh, Wyche, no. On the contrary.'

'By the way, I do not serve bacon in this house. But you can have pig's tongue. I slice it into rashers and fry them in an oil which I extract from the skins of snails. Cute, don't you think?'

Harris's stomach was churning. All of a sudden he didn't fancy breakfast any more. 'Yeah. Delicious. But...'

'Fine. Now you make yourself comfortable, Mr Harris, and I'll away and prepare the liver,' she ended, turning away from the table.

'Eh... excuse me, Mrs Wyche, but I think I... '

She stopped at the kitchen door. 'Mr Harris, has anyone ever told you that you bear an uncanny likeness to Omar Sharif?'

Not that again, Harris thought. 'As a matter of fact, most people do,' he replied with a smile.

'Strange.'

'What is?' he asked.

'According to the television news, Omar Sharif died in his sleep last night.'

Harris had a relatively successful first day at the office. The department in which he worked was a colourful palette of hues and shades: a few dark tones, several soft tints of greyness, an assortment of creamy delights and an admixture of transparency and thickness.

It became clear, however, that things were not all as they seemed. One employee in particular, a Madeline Dayford-Knight, caught his interest. She would be in her late twenties, of wistful character with no pretentions in personal fashion. Upon dining with this self-declared white magician over sticky toffee pudding in the company's canteen, he learned more of the weird and wonderful landlady back at the B & B. Madeline had known Mrs Wyche for many years. He learnt of her penchant for 'mystical feasts', sexual fantasies with the living dead, of drug-induced orgies with spectres and fairies and her inner knowledge of seagulls' behavioural instincts. Madeline grimly warned the newcomer of the woman, who she said was better known in these parts as Madame Astoroth.

'I've seen it all before,' Harris commented, as they took their lunch trays to the kitchen hatch.

'But you've never been up here before,' she replied. 'I'm warning you, Wilson, be careful.'

Harris was back in his room at the guest house by 5.15pm. The rain had already started and, to his utter bewilderment, the snoring was still in full flow. But it was louder, much louder than before, of a higher stridency; shrieking.

There was a soft knock on the door.

'Just a minute,' said Harris. He got up from the bed and straightened his tie before opening the door. 'Ah, Mrs Wyche,' he said with a forced smile.

She was dressed in a purple robe with a crimson rope belt tied around her waist. Around her neck was a gold chain on which was hooked a silver pentacle. Her hair was back-combed, evocative in the way it seemed to stand on end, the eyes circled with mascara, as if it had been painted on in a hurry, the face shrunken and ghoulish. Were those bloodstains on her fingertips?

'Mr Harris, you'll want dinner now, I presume?' she rasped.

'Eh, well, to tell you the truth, I'm not... '

'Fine. Shall we say fifteen minutes?'

'Look, Mrs Wyche, I'm not really hungry and, besides...
'

'Fifteen minutes, Mr Harris,' she retorted in a more urgent tone. She closed the door firmly.

Snoring, snoring, snoring. The sound was almost

overwhelming, and a dilemma now. He had turned down the offer of breakfast, much to the chagrin of Mrs Wyche. Who wouldn't have? But he couldn't stay in this room. It was getting stuffy and clammy, and he was convinced he'd seen 'things' during the night. And the calamity next door? What was going on in that room? Was it a tape recording? And if it was - why? No, there was nothing for it, he had to defer to the landlady's wishes. After all, it's only food, he said to himself aloud.

Before leaving for dinner he took three huge gulps of whisky straight from a bottle he'd purchased earlier at a nearby off-licence. That had the immediate effect of steadying his nerves.

The black cat was curled up in a ball at the top of the stairs.

'Hi, moggy,' he mumbled.

The big tom immediately looked up at the guest, its eyes frozen and fixed on his. In the semi-darkness Harris was momentarily entranced. It seemed to squawk in a quasi feline-cum-human voice: *'Don't eat!'*

Harris shook his head and rubbed his eyes. The cat was as before, snuggled up in a ball, its head half hidden behind its tail. He made his way down the winding staircase.

A plume of frankincense wafted about the small dining room. A solitary candle burned at the table, the Victorian cutlery arranged perfectly around the place-mat. From concealed speakers, Mozart's *The Magic Flute* played. Harris at least appreciated Mrs Wyche's taste in music.

And then she appeared, floating towards him, carrying two crystal glasses filled to the brim with a dark, red fluid.

She handed him one. 'To health, to happiness and to the Lord!' she exclaimed.

Harris put the glass to his lips. What Lord? Which one? The bouquet was surprisingly sweet, cheerful in its essence. As he sipped on the glass, he noted her stare, a steely coldness, but the wine, if that was what it was, went down as smooth as silk. It was the most beautiful drink he'd ever tasted.

'Now, Mr Harris, you see my tastes in life are cultured. They are of a higher domain. Don't you agree?'

Maybe things were looking up. 'Absolutely. This is excellent! Is it French? Italian? Bulgarian maybe?'

'No,' she replied. She sipped some more. 'I call it Rosa Animus. It stimulates the red blood cells and awakens the power of the spine. Oh, don't worry, Mr Harris, you'll not get drunk on it.'

'No no no, Mrs Wyche, I wouldn't have thought that for one minute.'

'Good. Now you finish your drink and I'll serve dinner.'

She was about to return to the kitchen when he suddenly realised there was only one place set for dining.

'Excuse me, Mrs Wyche, you're not eating?'

'Oh, no, Mr Harris, I ate earlier. Just a little meat, a few scraps, in fact.' And then she was gone.

Harris tried to concentrate on the music, but the constant snoring took the edge off his appreciation of *The Magic Flute*. He looked into the glass and pondered, but there was no reflection.

How to get out of this? He didn't feel in the least bit hungry, but he didn't want to disappoint the landlady, despite what he'd learned about her from Madeline earlier in the day. The loneliness was eating away at his gut. Here he was, a Londoner, a stranger to these parts. He thought he'd seen and heard it all in London. Certainly, there was a profusion of goofballs down there but here he was right in the middle of something. It was that seagull's shit that had started it all, he mused.

The shadowy figure arrived with a decanter.

'Ah, Mr Harris, I see you've almost finished. Here, let me,' she ended, taking his glass. She topped it up almost to overflowing. 'Dinner will be served in five minutes.'

Harris couldn't smell anything. 'Well, I... don't think... '

'It's very special, Wilson. You don't mind if I call you Wilson, do you? It's just that I like to be on first name terms with my guests before they... depart.'

A freezing current slithered down Harris' back. 'No, eh... sorry, uh, no I don't mind.' He swallowed another mouthful of the liquid.

She turned on her heel before declaring with a wide grin across crimson lips, 'Madeline Dayford-Knight is a murderess. She hacked to pieces a whole family in Inverurie three years ago.'

Harris coughed and spluttered some of the wine down his neck-tie. This was weird, really fucking weird. 'I'm getting out of here,' he muttered to himself. But the action of standing up defeated him; his legs were as ingots of iron ore, his torso magnetised on the chair. A bead of sweat rolled down his temple. And the snoring was getting louder. But his hand moved effortlessly to lift the glass to his lips. It had a life of its own.

Mrs Wyche appeared, this time armed with a silver plate, which she placed down in front of her visitor. It bore salad. Lumps of greenery, red roots, brown, shiny leaves, a stodgy paste and what looked like tiny bones. Was that a bat's head, a fried wing? A red sauce with white specks?

'You're not feeling very well, Wilson?' She was at his side now, leaning over his shoulder, a fork in hand. 'Here,' she said stabbing one of the bones. 'Take this. It's good for you.'

Harris, in a muddled, confused state of mind, opened his mouth, zombie-like. And then another mouthful. More wine. The sauce with the white specks, the roots. More wine. Endless mouthfuls of God knows what. She fed him lovingly as a mother to her new-born child.

'I - can't - eat - any - more. Please,' he implored urgently.

She was now sitting opposite him, glancing directly into his eyes. She broke into a hellish, screeching laughter. To Harris's senses it merged horribly with the snoring of the occupant of the room upstairs. He sat motionless at the table, noting the blood which covered her tiny, blackened, but now, sharp teeth. And a pungent, acrid smell seemed to emanate from her breath, an odour he'd never sensed before.

The snoring was getting louder, but it was now more a snarling growl, and it was getting closer, ever closer. It was coming down the staircase. He knew it. It would be here any minute...

'Now, Mr Harris,' she began. Congealed blood was

dripping from her mouth and nose, running down her fragile neck and onto her robe. 'Now for your initiation, the Ceremony of Your Arrival.'

She took her glass of wine and spat blood into it, a green tincture, before beckoning him to come closer. The snarling, growling snore seemed to wrap itself around his body as if death itself had finally arrived. He could see the living dead feeding off each other all around him. Bloodied internal organs, entangled hair, rotten teeth, fleshy bones, half eaten. He couldn't help himself from throwing up everything he'd eaten during the past 24 hours. A black seagull appeared from nowhere, but it had the head of a gargoyle, screams of hell itself. The witch in front of him was now just skin and bone and blood, no eyes, no teeth, metamorphosing into Satan himself. His head swam in images of Hell, of monsters half-human, half-animal, screaming out for the termination of their suffering, the overwhelming heat of flames and conflagration...

Zummmmp! Silence. Pure and virginal silence. And then a voice, a voice of a woman. His eyes were heavy, every bone in his body numb, his vocal chords seized.

'Excuse me, sir? Excuse me?'

'Huh?' he managed.

'Sir, would you mind fastening your seat-belt? We'll be arriving at Aberdeen in ten minutes.'

Harris followed the last remaining passengers to the door of the aircraft. In front of him was a woman, sixtyish, greying hair and sophisticated in dress. It had been quite stuffy on the plane and he would welcome a breath of fresh air with open arms. Upon arriving at the door of the aircraft he took in a deep breath and at that point he heard the squawk of a bird overhead. Before stepping onto the metal staircase he looked up, waited for a moment as it swooped low, and immediately retracted his step. A huge, black dropping fell on the woman in front of him.

He knew he was going to have a nice day.

Confessions of a Bitter Angel

I wasn't sure if I was awake or still dreaming. I was aware of the sensation of my tongue searching around inside my mouth like some viperous snake exploring its nest after a midday snooze. The tongue had a life of its own, investigating cavities, molars, incisors, the palate, checking out if there were other occupiers of this cavern that was my arid mouth. A numbness prevailed, as my awareness of where I was broke through the alcoholic miasma of the night before. Yeah, it was always 'the night before' these days.

My head spun like a top, accompanied by a buzzing that seemed to zip between the anvils of my ears like a ping-pong ball, searing bolts of pain rendering my neck almost motionless. But above all, a nauseating churning in my stomach began the excruciating morning spasms of the hell that is alcoholism. I just made it to the bathroom in time as I threw up the previous day's food intake - and it wasn't much. What had I eaten yesterday? Too tired to think. Wait a minute - yeah, that's right, I had some toast with marmalade in the morning, but that was washed down with a half a bottle of cheap red wine from Asda. Lunch? Haven't a clue. Dinner? A sandwich? Yeah, that's it, a cheese and ham sandwich, again from Asda. I was sick again; just a greeny liquid, acid to the taste that caught the back of my throat.

I drank six glasses of water straight from the tap and washed my face. And then I caught sight of it in the mirror, something I always tried to avoid like the plague first thing in the morning.

It had been my birthday the previous week - 44 - and looking at that ogreish mug staring back at me in the mirror, I thought, yup, forty-four, but you look like sixty-four. Wrinkles the size of mountain precipices brought on by a lifetime of smoking 60 fags a day, facial skin that resembled the pelt of an undernourished goat and a pair of eyes so red and dead beat, eyes that might close forever soon and never see the light of day again.

I picked up the disposable razor, only to find it was broken. So, no shave today then. And as more spasms began to seize my stomach, I suddenly remembered I was to attend that AA meeting today. Man, I could murder a drink!

I went through to the kitchen and opened the fridge. There must have been about 20 cans of Carlsberg Special in there and apart from two bottles of unopened white wine, there was not one item of food to be seen, not a sausage. For the first time in a long time I suffered a prick of conscience.

The man at the AA had said nobody would get in if they smelt of booze. I had the can in one hand and the ring-pull in the other. To pull or not to pull, that was the question...

Fuck it! I ripped off the ring-pull and gulped down half the can. Ahhhhhh! I wiped my lips with the back of my hand. That was so good - so refreshing. The other half of the can I finished in another gulp. There. Finished. Done. Finito!

Without further ado I raided the fridge again and opened another can. Where were my cigarettes? Alcoholism and memory loss - they went hand-in-hand in my life, like Laurel and Hardy. Sometimes I couldn't remember what I'd done a few hours before. Names of peoples, places, whole segments of my life, seemed to have been obliterated by that devastating weapon of man's destruction: alcohol.

My trusty pack of Marlboro was sitting face down on a plate of unfinished baked beans on toast. How did they end up there? God knows. Must have been the night before, but I didn't remember opening the tin. I lit up a cigarette and took my lager through to the lounge. Shit! Stuff everywhere. I slumped down on the sofa and flicked on the television - daytime telly - some soap actress being grilled by the customary husband-and-wife team. The smiles forced, the questions well-rehearsed, the polished nails, stylish hairdos, sickening to watch.

What was sobering, however, were the two near-empty whisky bottles on my coffee table, and empty lager cans, some lying on their sides, others squeezed shapeless. I was just too tired to bother. Maybe tomorrow I'll bring out the

Hoover, the polish and dusters, clean the place up. Yeah, clean the flat; it'll be a spiritual exercise, cleansing the spirit, washing away the drink, this evil dependency on beer and brandy, whisky and wine - fuck, everything!

It was then that I looked at my trousers and shirt, the ones I had worn the previous day - had I worn them the day before that? There was certainly a ripe pungency emanating from my armpits. Yes, a long hot bath - that would do the trick.

On the way through to the bathroom, I came to a stop at the kitchen door. The fridge gripped my sense of taste as a sensual magnet. I could do with another drink; maybe have a lager whilst running the bath. Great idea. And that was exactly what I was going to do.

And then, the doorbell went. Bzzzzz. Bzzzzz. Bzzzzz.

Shit, who could that be? I couldn't recall when I'd last had a visitor. My mind flicked through the index book of possibilities: old Mrs Barnes next door, the paper boy, Asda delivery man (nope, couldn't be that - hadn't ordered any drink from them today), postman?

Bzzzzz. Bzzzzz. Bzzzzz.

I sneaked over to the drawn curtains of the lounge and peered out. It was Kellie! What did she want? I looked around the room; Christ! Ignore her, I thought, just ignore her. Bzzzzz. Bzzzzz. Bzzzzz. Then she was at the lounge window, her head bobbing from side to side. What to do?

I put the can of lager in the fridge and went through to the front door. I stood there, my trembling hand making for the door knob. To hell with it - I opened the door.

Kellie's smile turned to stone as she gazed into my eyes. God knows what she saw. My head slumped a little and I averted my gaze momentarily.

'Sean?'

She looked as gorgeous as she ever had. It was the first time I'd seen her in over two years, even though she lived just a mile down the road. Always well turned out, classy, clean-looking, and was that a hint of Chanel No 5 in the air? That was always her favourite.

'Hi, Kellie,' I eventually said.

She looked over my shoulder. 'How are you?'

I must have smelt like a distillery. 'Okay, I guess.' Should I ask her in?

'This came for you today,' she said, handing over a buff-coloured, official-looking A4 envelope.

'Thanks,' I replied. What was this?

Her faced softened a bit. 'Well, can I come in?'

'Uh, yes, yeah, I suppose so.'

She brushed past me and stood at the door to the lounge. Her head panned around the room like a movie camera, slow and deliberate. I was behind her. In a way I wanted to try and see what she was witnessing. She put herself down on a chair next to the television. There was some chap on dressed in a military uniform banging on about Islamist terrorism. I walked over and turned down the volume.

Kellie was still assessing the domestic anarchy that confronted her when I sat down on the sofa. I was anxious to look her straight in the eye, because after 11 years of marriage I still felt that I loved her.

'Some things never change, I see,' she eventually said. It wasn't a malicious statement, just one from the heart.

I still couldn't look at her. 'It's my life, Kellie. I'm living my life the way I want to. Know what I mean?'

'Anything you say, Sean.'

'Sorry about the mess. I was just getting ready to clean the place up,' I lied.

'If you say so.' She paused and looked about the floor. 'Oh, Sean, look at you. Look about you. You're going to kill yourself. Why? The last time I spoke to you; remember? We'd been divorced a month, remember at Jill's fortieth?'

'Remember it well.'

'You were going to turn over a new leaf. Remember?'

I did remember. It was a great night. There would be one last bash, then I'd give up drinking for good. But that leaf's vibrant verdancy changed very quickly into a raw oatmeal colour, shrivelled up into a crisp that would easily be crushed underfoot.

'You know where I'm going today?'

'Don't tell me - Alcoholics Anonymous?' she offered sarcastically.

'Yup!'

That alluring smile returned to her lips. 'You're joking!'

'I am. Five o'clock. Guess where?' I asked.

'Dunno!'

'St Luke's community hall.'

'There?'

'Yup. Great, isn't it. I might even see the Light.' I could have managed to finish off that lager. Should I offer her some tea? Did I have I any milk? No, the fridge was bare except for booze.

'Well, good for you. So is this part of a course or what?' she asked.

'In fact it will be my first time. I'm nervous.' I brought up my arms parallel with my shoulders. 'You see, I've got the DTs, the ultimate mark of the alcoholic.' I lit up another cigarette from the stub of the last one.

'And you're still not working?' she asked.

'Living on my overdraft.' I looked her straight in the eye. 'I still love you, Kellie.' The words seemed to escape from some deep vault of my mind reserved for 'unwanted memories.'

Kellie smiled again. 'Oh, Sean,' she sighed.

'Sorry, I didn't mean that.' I got to my feet. 'Maybe you should be going?'

Surprisingly she remained on the chair. 'I was seeing someone else - up until last week,' she said. She bit her lip. 'It just fell to pieces.'

'Oh?' The thought suddenly struck me; should I offer her a glass of wine? 'Did you love him, Kellie?'

She paused. This time it was her turn to look away. 'Yes. I think I did.'

'Want to tell me about it?'

And then, suddenly, she got to her feet. 'Anyway, I came round to deliver that letter. I need to get back to the office. Rushed off our feet at the moment.'

She was at the door of the lounge. I was inches away from grasping her hand, but thought better of it. So vulnerable, so innocent. But I couldn't help myself. Then she turned to me and gazed into my eyes. How many times had I bathed my heart in those dreamy eyes of hers? I flung my arms around her and pulled her in tight. To my utter astonishment, she did likewise.

'Kellie, darling, I still love you so much.'

I was conscious of her sniffling and then she suddenly burst into tears. She pulled away from me. 'I... I must be going, now, Sean.'

'But, Kellie.'

She had the front door opened, the tears streaking down her cheeks, eyes awash with tears. 'Maybe see you some other time.'

And then she was gone.

Why did I let her leave? Damn! Always making the wrong decisions. As I shut the door, her footfalls fell away in the distance. I closed the door and locked it; couldn't be too careful, with the spate of break-ins around these parts in recent times.

I returned to the lounge and lit another cigarette. What to do next? That buff envelope was lying on the coffee table, but I just wasn't interested. These days the only mail I opened was the stuff from the gas, electricity or telephone companies. The rest I tended to throw in the bucket or leave in a pile by the front door.

The fridge was calling me again and, once more, I opened a Carlsberg Special and brought it through to the lounge. There was some weather report on the television informing us that rain was forecast for late afternoon. Huh, another shitty, rainy day in Paradise, I thought. Then I impulsively went over to the dressing table. Pictures. Yeah, photographs, Kellie and me. I put down my can and sifted through the drawers. Yup, loads of Photo Factory envelopes, all crumpled and dog-eared, as were some of the photos I immediately removed. I took a pile of the envelopes and sat myself down on the sofa.

And there, as good as gold, were the many pictures I had taken of Kellie over the years. I selected one - it was taken on the steps leading up to the Hotel Paris in Monte Carlo. She had bought this turquoise chiffon dress the previous day from a very expensive designer boutique in Nice. I had always loved her in that dress, cut at the knee, the way it wafted in a gentle breeze - oh how much I loved to photograph her in it! And then another photo - this one taken in some shopping mall in Hong Kong the previous year. Kellie wore that mesmeric smile that oozed sex and that was probably why I loved shooting her so much. Then that wonderful day spent on Lantau Island, photographing her at the Buddhist temple, she lighting Patchouli incense sticks outside, and then a giggly, diminutive Chinese lady who took our picture. So much in love, I thought.

I picked out the photo I had taken outside the city hall after her PhD graduation ceremony. The number of nights she'd burnt the midnight oil writing that thesis. And I guess that's when it had all gone downhill. She'd spend countless hours in the study, the tap-tap-tapping of the computer keys seeming to stretch into early morning. Then up at the crack of dawn, more study, note-taking, the endless lectures she attended during night classes. And for what? A measly piece of embossed card that would demonstrate to the world just how intellectual she was.

But I was an intellectual, too. I had two engineering degrees, was a member of three professional institutions, had written research papers on exotic metals - I once *was* somebody. And now... yeah, just where was I now?

I woke with a start. The television was still playing - it was kids' cartoons - Andy Pandy. My gaze fell on the five empty cans of Carlsberg. I had passed out! Then my watch told me it had just gone four o'clock. Shit, I had that AA meeting at five. A squeaky voice told me not to go. I could just sit down here in front of the TV and get drunk - well, more drunk. But a sterner tone of voice told me to get to the AA - in fact the voice had a similarity to that of Kellie's. Was she working some mental control on me? After all, she was a well-qualified psychologist and mentalist.

I decided to have a quick shower. Now what to wear to this AA thing? Instead of thinking too much about it, I threw on a denim shirt and jeans, and eased into my trainers. Bugger it, they'll just have to accept me as I was. Now, should I have a small snifter before I left? Why not? In fact I downed two more Carlsbergs and three shots of whisky before I left. The rest of the Scotch I poured into my hip-flask. Nerves? No nerves. I felt as though I could take on Mike Tyson and hammer him into the canvas. Bold as brass! As cold as steel! That was me!

The taxi dropped me outside St Luke's community hall.

After paying the driver, I stood at the wrought-iron gates of the church. Commuters rushing to catch buses brushed past me and all of a sudden I got the jitters. This was crazy; where had that hardened resolve gone?

I opened the gates and walked up the path leading to the hall that was attached to the side of the church. There was a light on, and as I approached I could hear the echo of voices inside. I quietly opened the door of the hall and stepped inside. The doors to the hall were slightly ajar and I could see perhaps eight people sitting in a semi-circle with this bearded chap standing in the centre. He was banging on about his previous life as an alcoholic, but it was his tone of voice, shrill, cutting, dispassionate. I automatically took one, two, three swigs of the hip-flask. Now then, that resulted in an immediate flash of certainty. Buoyed the spirit, I sauntered into the hall.

Suddenly the 'beard' stopped talking, the rest of the group turning their heads in unison.

'Ah, Sean, come on in, it's nice to see you.'

The other alcoholics just sort of sat there, bums glued to seats, gazing at me as if their worst nightmare had just barged in on their little worlds. I felt unsteady on my feet, which was unusual for me because that's one aspect of my drinking that never affected me - I just never swayed about, walking as if I had two right feet. The Beard's smile metamorphosed into a steely grin as I made my way towards the group. His eyes followed me as a submarine's periscope would track an enemy warship. One of the group was sniffing the air, and the Beard was beginning to regard me with some unease.

I began to pick my way around this sorry-looking half circle of dipsomaniacs, these pink elephants whose gaunt looks and dishevelled appearance made me feel worse. Shit, I thought I was coming here to be uplifted, but this bunch of no-hopers was beginning to make me feel physically sick.

And then one of them, a 50-something skeletal specimen sporting a ripped tweed jacket and corduroy trousers that looked as though they hadn't been washed in years, turned to me and stated, 'Hey guv, you've been drinkin'!'

The Beard coughed nervously and asked, 'Is that true, Sean?'

Silly bastard - of course it was true. I'd been drinking solidly nearly all day. My breath must have smelt like a cross between a Holstein brewery and a Black Label distillery. I stopped in my tracks, removed my hip flask and knocked back a couple of shots. That drew several gasps from the bums on seats. And then I went into a fit of laughter. It wasn't the booze - no, it was the sheer look of amazement on those pathetic phizogs.

'Sean, sit down, please,' the Beard ordered. 'Look, we're all in the same boat here; can't you see that - I'm - we're here to help.'

Well that did it for me. In that moment something deep inside me cracked; it was as if someone had wrenched the very guts from my insides and thrown them on the floor. It wasn't what the Beard said, it wasn't those faces now viewing me like an audience at a horror movie; no, it was something I couldn't put my finger on.

'See this?' I began, withdrawing the hip flask from my

jacket pocket. 'This has been my life for fifteen years. For fifteen fucking dead years, this has kept me from going insane. Fifteen years of pissing it up against a wall, getting plastered into oblivion, fighting the demons, little embryonic monsters that infiltrated my soul and evolved into terrible nightmares. That's what drink did for me.' I began gesticulating with my hands, the anger in my words that were like flaming swords aimed not so much at those in the hall, but more at myself. 'Because you see, folks, I lost my marriage, the very bedrock on which I built my life, my prosperity, my happiness, her happiness, our happiness. Why didn't I listen to my wife's calls, her concerns, the endless fights we had? And all because I had turned from a loving husband to a callous drunkard.'

'But, Sean, we all have crosses to bear...'

'Shut the fuck up!' I screamed. Then I began aiming my rhetoric at these bums on the seats. And as I looked deeply into each of those faces, those dead, weary eyes, I felt a strength of purpose welling up in me. It was as if I was winning back my soul. 'Drunks!' I exclaimed, looking at them in turn. 'Pisspots! Winos! Piss artists! Do you want to face the rest of your lives walking around with these labels? Because you will. Tonight I have decided I don't want to have this label any more. There's only one label I want nailed to the headboard of my bed tonight and that's the one that reads 'Freedom' - liberated from selfishness because that is the second biggest enemy after booze - the want to put ourselves before anybody or anything else. Because when we get pissed we shut up the doors leading to freedom. We close the gates that take us from humanity to animalism. And for what?'

I aimed that last question at the Beard himself. But he just stood there, his chin resting slightly on his chest, his eyes fixed on the floorboards of this church hall.

I tossed aside the hip flask, turned on my heel and made my way to the door. There was total silence in the hall. Stopping at the door, I looked back at the group. Eight heads were turned in my direction. The Beard smiled and waved...

Outside the air smelt fresh and clean. It smelt different, almost scented, although this was surely the same air I had smelt when I had got off the bus a half-hour earlier. And as I set off down the path to the wrought-iron gates, my attention was drawn to a shiny object on the grass verge to my right. I stooped down and picked up a rosary. The beads were of green emerald linked onto a gold chain. The crucifix was of solid gold, about the length of my pinkie, and the figure of Jesus was etched in magnificent detail. I held it in my hand for a moment - was this some kind of sign? I instinctively looked heavenward, then I clutched the rosary and slipped it into my jacket pocket and made my way to the bus stop.

My flat was chilly, and I momentarily shivered as I stepped inside. Maybe it was the drink wearing off or something, but instead of making for the fridge, I went through to the kitchen and put on the electric kettle. For the first time in ages I felt like a cup of tea. Yes, an old-fashioned cuppa.

Wait a minute, did I have any sugar, teabags? I opened the cupboard above the fridge. Yup - both.

It was when I was dropping a teabag into the cup that my eye caught sight of the envelope that Kellie had brought around earlier. What was it, anyway? Well, it was very officious-looking, whatever it was. Probably a bill - but it didn't look like one. Junk mail? I decided to wait until my tea was ready before opening it.

I took my cup of tea through to the lounge. But before I opened the envelope I went into my jacket and withdrew the rosary. Then that feeling of peace washed over me again, a relaxedness that was welcomed like the cup of tea I was about to drink.

I drank some of the tea; it tasted slightly acid, but that was probably due to the alcoholic savaging my taste buds had been subjected to over the years. Now, the envelope. I slid my thumb along the edge and took out the letter. I immediately recognised the logo of our local technical college - it was now a polytechnic, whatever that meant.

I had to read and re-read the words several times before it finally sank in: *'...please confirm your attendance for the interview on July 7th'.*

A job!

Now what was Kellie's number, I asked myself as I lifted the receiver. Let me think... ah yes. I punched in the six digit number, reading the letter again.

'Hello?'

'Hi, Kellie, it's Sean!'

There was a moment's silence. 'Hey, this'll have to stop... us talking twice in the same day.'

'Listen, listen,' I enthused, 'Remember I spent a couple of years at the Techie trying to teach those uninterested buggers mechanical engineering?'

'Uh-huh. You mean the letter I brought around?'

'Yup, I've just opened it. I've got to attend an interview in two weeks' time. Seems they have a new intake of Saudi students - you know it's to do with that exchange scheme run by the Chamber of Commerce? Well, they can't get lecturers for love nor money and they're asking previous employees if they'd like to sign up as part-time lecturers with a possibility of full-time employment within the first year. It's great news, Kellie!'

'Oh, that's great news,' she said. And she sounded as if she really meant it. 'But?' Her tone changed to one of apprehension.

'I've quit drinking.' And there it was. It was as if it were someone else saying the words and I was a bystander. 'Honest, Kellie, I have really quit!' Again. Were these my actual words? I had to look at my hands, touch my face, to comprehend if this were real - not a drunken stupor. A dream. But I was saying these words. It was me, nobody else, they were my words.

'You used to tell me that every other day, Sean.'

'Let me prove it. Give me another chance and I'll prove it!'

Again there was a deathly silence between us. 'Hello?' I asked.

'When's your interview again?'

I picked up the rosary and felt a warm glow from the crucifix. Maybe someone up there liked me after all.

Time for another nice cup of tea.

The Beadle

The Reverend Jacob Abrams was sitting on a small, moth-eaten leather sofa that looked to have seen better days. The old vicar, who was well past retirement age, brushed a hand through his silvery, bushy beard. His tired eyes were transfixed on the great holy book that was opened at Exodus 20:3-17. He read, *'For in six days the LORD made the heavens and the earth, the sea, and all that is in them, but he rested on the seventh day. Therefore the LORD blessed the Sabbath day and made it holy.'*

As he said the last word, a massive, thunderous roar crashed onto the roof of the small cottage, shaking the building to its foundations. A shard of lightning momentarily threw the darkened room into brilliant silvery light, crisp and clean. The old man closed his eyes, made the sign of the cross over his tweed waistcoat and uttered some words. He had to remind himself that it was actually

Sunday and the mahogany grandfather clock's brass hands showed eleven-thirty.

The darkness outside was permeated with crashing downfalls of autumn rain battering against the window. He rose from his seat and slowly walked over to the window, then stopped midway - it was that pain in his back again. Damn it, why wouldn't it go away?

Another rumble of thunder ensued and more sheets of rain hammered against the window. Peering at the glass, he hardly recognised his wrinkled reflection, gaunt features. In that moment, for the first time in years, he had to admit that he was an old, old man. His bloodshot eyes stared back at him.

And then another tremendous lightning bolt crashed off the window and his ashen face instantly transformed into a skeletal visage, haunting, frightening. He put his hand to his face but there was nothing there, no skin, bone, skull, sinew - nothing. 'Lord God!' he exclaimed, 'why me, Lord?' More thunder and lightning, great sheets of rain against the window, and it was as if the little building was about to collapse on top of him. As he continued to stare at the baleful face in the window, it suddenly began to transform into his own aged features.

And then... complete silence. He turned around slowly. The half-burnt candle glowed softly in the far corner of the room next to his overloaded bookshelves. Utter stillness bathed the room, except for the monotonous tick-tock of the grandfather clock. What sounded like the howl of a wolf echoed from the distance as he sat back down on the sofa.

He lifted the Bible onto his lap, opened it and donned his horn-rimmed spectacles.

'Place your problems in God's hands and have faith that He will do the impossible in your life. The LORD shall fight for you, and ye shall hold your peace.'

The vicar smiled contentedly and sighed. Yes, he knew a lifetime of prayer and dedication would protect him from all harm.

Suddenly his soliloquy was disturbed by loud thuds on the door of the cottage. He turned and listened. Bang, bang, bang, bang! It was almost insane in its urgency. Who could that be at this time of the night? Bang, bang, bang, bang, once more!

'I'm coming, I'm coming!' he shouted as he got to his feet. 'Who is it? Who is there?'

Bang, bang, bang, bang!

'Okay, okay!'

He opened the door, and there stood the figure of Ronald Granger, the beadle, soaked to the skin, face scrawny and gangling. In church he was the vicar's right-hand man, but now he seemed different.

'Come in, Ronnie,' the vicar said. Granger followed the vicar into the room. The beadle stood there in a trance, his eyes wide and staring. He had aged since the last time they had been together, which had been only the previous morning. And those eyes, staring, unmoving...

'Ronnie, what's happened? I don't understand.'

The beadle remained standing like some medieval marble column in a faraway land. He eventually looked down at the vicar and growled, 'The devil led him to

Jerusalem and had him stand on the highest point of the temple. If you are the Son of God, throw yourself down from here.'

'Huh?' the vicar asked. 'Ronnie, maybe you are feeling poorly?'

The beadle yelled, 'The Devil led him up to a high place and showed him in an instant all the kingdoms of the world. Look at you! You pride yourself as being without sin when we are the Devil's children!' He ground his teeth, rainwater continuing to drip from his suede cap, and yet he remained static.

The vicar continued to gaze up at the beadle. He concentrated his gaze and asked fervently, 'Ron, why are you talking like this? The Devil? I don't understand.'

'Depart from me, you who are cursed!' the beadle roared, and then, almost as if chanting from some arcane religious ceremony, 'And go into the eternal fire prepared for the Devil and his angels!'

The old vicar at that point tried to rise from his seat, but couldn't. He stretched and wobbled in the sofa, but remained rooted to the spot. And then the beadle began laughing, again in a psychotic, distressing tongue: 'Behold the Redeemer, the Anti-Christ, who stands before you in awesome glory and diabolical majesty. Look at thee, sinner, who speaks as though the demon-God lives within thy soul - be away with you!'

The Reverend Jacob Abrams woke from his slumber. He looked up at the grandfather clock through a half-opened eye. The clock showed thirteen minutes to ten. A beam of sunlight illuminated the small room. He looked around the room and then stared down at the floor. Had he just wakened from a bad dream? What had Ronnie been talking about? Was he drunk? Had it actually been Ron?

He lifted up the Bible from the table and thumbed through to the Book of Revelation. He began ruminating about the book, and how it spanned three literary genres: the epistolary, the apocalyptic, and the prophetic. He recalled it beginning with John, on the island of Patmos in the Aegean Sea, and about the addressing of a letter to the Seven Churches of Asia. He remembered it describing a series of prophetic visions, including figures such as the Whore of Babylon and the Beast, culminating in the Second Coming of Jesus Christ. So what was that he had experienced last night? Was it last night? And where was Ronnie?

The holy book reclaimed his attention. *'He was given power to give breath to the image of the first beast, so that it could speak and cause all who refused to worship the image to be killed. He also forced everyone, small and great, rich and poor, free and slave, to receive a mark on his right hand or on his forehead, so that no-one could buy or sell unless he had the mark, which is the name of the beast or the number of his name. This calls for wisdom. If anyone has insight, let him calculate the number of the beast, for it is man's number. His number is 666.'* He paused for a moment. Ronald - the Beast?

As he muttered the last words, thunder and lightning

once again arrived from nowhere, accompanied by semi-darkness. He lit the candle once more and repeated, 'His number is 666.' The thunderstorm raged overhead and once again the small cottage was caught in the heavenly rage. It was almost as if the number of the Devil had instigated in a damnable way the storm overhead.

He fell to his knees, clutched the large bronze cross he wore around his neck and began to pray. Something was amiss; it was as if he was in the middle of a diabolical lesson whose message was indecipherable. He stood up and tottered over to the window, next to which was a shelf with yesterday's *Daily Mail* newspaper. Something caught his eye on the masthead. It was the date, today's date: 20th June 1966.

The sixth month of the year 1966!

Another massive thunderclap rang out overhead, more heavy rain, lightning. It was as if Hell had arrived, unannounced. And somewhere in the distance, intermingled with all the fury, the sound of church bells.

The vicar stared into the window again, only this time his face seemed interchanged with that of the beadle. It was like a carousel of ghostly images, one moment himself, the next Ronald Granger.

He closed his eyes and an indistinct voice declared: 'Go to the church, please go to the church, you are needed in the church.' The voice was pleading, as if the person was about to be executed or undergo some other terrible fate.

'What? Who are you?' he shouted, turning around. His head was spinning, but he found himself walking over to the closet and pulling on his boots and overcoat.

'Go to the church,' the voice beseeched. 'The answer is there waiting for you!'

As soon as the vicar had banged the cottage door shut behind him, he was soaked by huge pellets of thundering rainwater. The storm seemed to intensify as soon as he turned to his left to walk up the tree-lined lane to the church, about 50 yards away. Thunder and lightning exploded overhead and he pondered that maybe this was a bad idea, this preposterous journey up the small hilly lane to his place of worship. The rain hammered down ferociously, little muddy streams of rainwater splashing on his boots.

Pausing for a moment, he gazed up at the church, this great shrine from which he took comfort in times of trouble and faithlessness. Now the church bells tolled even louder, as if beckoning him to come quickly, as if something depended on his presence.

By the time he was halfway up the lane his mind was a carousel of contradictory thoughts, of Ronnie, archangels, the Devil, of hymns, psalms, Christ, of high days, holidays, schooldays, thoughts of music, magic, incense; the carousel of memories and emotions whirred around his head at the speed of sound...

At last he arrived at the open gates to the church to stare at the open door as if beckoning him in, and for what purpose - why? He wiped his soaking face with a hanky and stepped up to the door. His silvery beard was saturated with rainwater. He turned his head and listened and in that moment, the storm that had guided him to this point transformed into the beatific harmony of the church organ. All contagious thoughts and emotions died in an instant, his heart mellowing and ethereal tones of solemnity filling his very soul.

He stepped into the church. Perhaps half-way down the aisle there was a female form seated on a pew, head facing forwards. Who was this?

He quietly walked down towards her and as he arrived at her side, the music stopped abruptly. The woman, as if on cue, turned to the vicar. He gazed down at her. She was dressed in black and wearing a transparent black veil.

'Betty!' said vicar, 'what are you doing here?'

She looked up at him, a solitary tear rolling down an ashen cheek. 'So sudden, vicar,' she eventually murmured.

The vicar sat on a pew opposite. 'Betty, I mean, why are you here? Is Ronnie coming?'

She wiped a tear from her eye. 'We had thirty-three good years, vicar. Never a bad word was spoken. A heart of gold. The most amazing fellow you could ever meet on a day's march.'

The vicar leaned closer, trying and failing to make sense of her words. 'Where's Ronnie?' he asked.

The church was in complete silence. Betty gazed up ahead to the statue of the Virgin Mary next to the pulpit. 'Such innocence!' she exclaimed, and then she began to cry.

The vicar got up from his pew, stepped over and put a comforting arm around her shoulder. 'Betty, what's happened? Is it Ronnie?'

She began to weep. 'I never saw it coming. So sudden.

He passed away yesterday. The police found him curled up on the path to our house. He was clutching a Bible, vicar, and it was opened up at Revelation. The initials J.A. were scribbled on the page in black ink.'

The Reverend Jacob Abrams look down at the wooden floor. His attention was drawn to a small ant ambulating across the floorboards.

So who was the man who had visited him yesterday?